Alpha King

A Dark Paranormal Academy Romance

Wolf Ridge High

Renee Rose

Renee Rose Romance

Want FREE Renee Rose books?

Go to http://subscribepage.com/alphastemp to sign up for Renee Rose's newsletter and receive a free copy of *Alpha's Temptation, Theirs to Protect, Owned by the Marine* and more. In addition to the free stories, you will also get bonus epilogues, special pricing, exclusive previews and news of new releases.

Chapter One

*L*auren

I wake soaked in sweat. One of the many downsides to living in Arizona.

Even now, in mid-September, the daily temperatures are above one hundred degrees. I can't. Freaking. Sleep.

I attempt to throw the covers off my body, but they tangle around my legs, making me thrash and kick like a mermaid caught in a net. The T-shirt I'm wearing clings to me.

I'm not the only one in this house still awake. In the room next door, my twin, Lincoln plays his electric guitar, sans amplification. I hear him jamming, still trying to master Eric Clapton's song, "Layla".

From the kitchen comes the sound of ice dropping into a glass. Our dad is up, too. We're a family of insomniacs.

I probably can't blame the heat. This is a hard week for all of us.

Anniversaries suck.

Still, cooler temperatures supposedly enable better sleep, so I swing my legs over the side of the bed to get up. The thermostat just outside my bedroom door reads seventy-two, which should be plenty cool, but I knock it down a few more degrees.

When I get back to my bedroom, I yank my damp shirt off and toss it on the floor. Maybe sleeping in nothing but my panties will work.

I walk over to the bank of windows that offers a view of the foothills. The full moon backlights the saguaro cacti, which stand like sentinels on the steep hillside.

I reach for the curtains to pull them closed then freeze.

The breath sticks in my throat.

The biggest wolf I've ever seen is outside my window, just twenty feet away.

Silver with white markings, he gleams in the light of the full moon. The beast is so illuminated, I can see the color of its eyes–ice blue.

I force an exhale from my lungs.

Now I know I'm not crazy. For the past several weeks, I've caught movement in the brush when I look out my window. Flashes of silver or the flick of a tail.

I guess I should be impressed. Mother Nature led an endangered animal right outside my bedroom window. For some reason, it just pisses me off though. Like the heat and the redneck bullies at my high school, having wild animals peering in my window feels like an intrusion. Another sign we don't belong here.

We should leave Wolf Ridge and go back to Manhattan.

The wolf stares at me. There's something challenging in its glare. Like he's the alpha, and I'm some young upstart he wants to put in her place.

My mom would've loved seeing this. She adored Arizona. Loved being surrounded by nature. But she's not here, which means this wolf sighting is a damn waste.

I unlock the window and shove it open.

"What are you looking at?" I shout at the wolf.

His upper lip curls in a growl.

I should be afraid. I should feel something, anything.

But I don't.

These days, I never do.

"*Shoo.*" I flick my hand in a dismissive gesture. "Go on. Get out of here."

I see a flash of gleaming white teeth.

Hear a ferocious snarl then the snap of powerful jaws.

I swear I barely blink before my window is obliterated by silver fur. The window screen bows inward and tears down the middle as the wolf's great body slams up against the frame.

I scream, frozen in place. I'm unable to move or look away.

Finally, I feel something beyond the out-of-body numbness. My body recognizes real danger. *And I love it.*

After feeling dead for so long, I relish the terror. The sensation of living. The return of emotion, even though it's a primitive one.

I lock eyes with the snarling wolf, almost daring it to come through that screen and eat me alive.

But then, just as quickly as it came, the wolf wheels around and lopes off into the woods, disappearing from sight.

* * *

Abe

No human should have such a glorious set of tits.

Even now, with a boot pressed to my throat, I'm

thinking about how Lauren Sterling looked with the moon's pale light illuminating her bare breasts.

Remembering the impudent upward tilt of her nipples. The sweet round underbellies. Thinking about what it would be like to fill my hands with them at the same time I'm breathing in that candy apple scent of hers.

"You want to explain why I just got a call from the Sterling mansion saying a rabid wolf tried to *attack their daughter?*" the sheriff snarls.

I'm flat on my back, showing my belly to Alpha Green and Sheriff Gleason.

Fuck.

I am so screwed right now.

I shift back to human form to speak, which only adds to my ignominious position. Now my dong is hanging out while I'm under the alpha's boot.

"I'm sorry, Alpha."

"*Sorry* doesn't cut it, son. You broke code."

My dad appears beside the other two men, and a familiar sensation of queasiness slithers in my stomach. He's going to freak out if he thinks I have the hots for a human.

I don't. I definitely don't.

My brain whirls as I try to figure my way out of this. The truth is—I don't know what happened. I don't know what keeps drawing me to the Sterling mansion—the opulent monstrosity on Moongaze Hill that abuts pack land and has a view of our roaming ground. The house where Lauren and her twin moved for their senior year.

It doesn't make sense that my wolf would be fascinated by a human.

All I know is I saw the ice princess from Manhattan— my stuck-up lab partner in chemistry—standing topless in her window.

Yes, *topless.*

I saw her gorgeous breasts, and I was unable to move or look away.

And then I realize–that's the answer. The plain truth, minus the part where I lost control, and my wolf lunged for her.

"I'm sorry, sir—I don't know what happened. I guess it was the hormones. I saw her naked in the window—"

"*Naked?*" My dad interrupts in disbelief.

"Yes, sir. She came to the window naked, and I don't know what happened. It must've been the full moon bringing on my alpha aggression. The next thing I knew I had lunged at the window. But I wasn't attacking her. I mean, I never meant to. I wouldn't hurt a human."

I might want to hold this particular one down and do dirty things to her, but I'm not going to tell my dad and the pack elders that.

"I see." The boot shifts from my throat to my chest, and I drag in a full breath. Some of the tension and blast of judgment leaves Alpha Green. "Hormones can do that to an alpha." There's a note of pride in his tone. Like we're talking, one alpha to another.

Suddenly, he's my mentor instead of a punisher.

"Son, you need to work some of that hormonal aggression out on the football field. Or if you need to get with a few human girls–not when the moon is full, of course–just to release some of your pent-up frustration–then you do it. Using protection, of course. Doesn't Coach Jamison talk to you boys about that sort of thing?"

"Yes, sir. Absolutely. But I don't need to f– *get* with a human. I've got things under control."

My dad would never forgive me for fucking a human. My whole life he's been telling my brother Austin and me we have to secure and maintain the position as alpha of our classes, so we can mate the female alpha. Ensure the family defect is never passed on.

"Do you, son? It doesn't seem that way from where I'm standing."

"Yes, sir. I don't know what happened tonight, but I swear it won't happen again."

"Make sure it doesn't," Alpha Green instructs. The boot eases back a little more.

"I will, sir."

Alpha Green removes his boot from my chest. "Now get up and get dressed. I'll sort out your problem with Sheriff Gleason."

"Thank you, sir. I'm sorry for the trouble I caused you and the pack."

I get up and give a dog-like shake before turning on my heel and walking out of the pack office.

My friends, Asher, J.J., Markley, and Sebs wait for me in the locker room. They're already dressed, and they're screwing around, playing the game where they throw a football as hard as they can at the other guy's face.

All four of them look at me expectantly, but I shake my head. No way I'm saying anything while still on pack property. Every shifter here has superhuman hearing, and no conversation goes undetected.

Of course, they all want to know what happened. I disappeared on the pack run, and when they came back, I was in the alpha's office.

I throw on shorts and a T-shirt, stuff my feet in a pair of flip-flops and head out to the dirt parking lot where my Range Rover is parked. The five of us pile in, and I start the truck. As soon as the last door slams shut, they're all talking at once.

"What up, Abe?" Markley croons from the front passenger seat.

"We heard you were at the Sterling mansion, supposedly attacking the Ice Princess. What did you do to her?" J. J. wants to know. He's the nice guy in our school pack. Senior Class President. Mr. Social. The guy I wish I could be. The guy I would be if I didn't have to maintain my position as alpha–a requirement set by my dad, not me.

"Tell me she was screaming because you finally got the frigid bitch—"

My wolf snarls. Before I can stop myself, I swing my arm sideways to slam my fist into the center of Markley's chest for disrespecting her.

Fuck.

Why would my wolf want to protect this human? She's never been anything but a snob to me.

Markley wheezes at the impact. "Sorry, bro."

In the rearview mirror, I see J.J. and Sebs exchange a look that makes me want to throat-punch both of them. I showed too much.

They think this human means something to me.

She doesn't. She definitely doesn't.

I would never screw around with a human. Especially not Lauren. The Ice Princess may be hot, her scent may do things to me, but there's absolutely nothing underneath that manicured, rich girl exterior.

It's a school night and late, so I don't drive back up to the mesa to light a fire and shoot the shit with the guys. This is the one time I don't want to hang out with my best friends because I know they're going to keep busting on me to figure out what happened tonight and why.

But I need to give them the story now because every

shifter kid at school tomorrow is going to want to know what happened, and my friends need to be the ones to spread it.

It has to be a story that puts me on the top. I'm the alpha of the school. I can't afford any perception of weakness. Especially not with my secret.

I pull up to Markley's house and kill the engine, then I twist around in my seat to see the guys. "Dude, she was naked. Standing in front of her bedroom window."

It makes my stomach queasy to talk about Lauren this way. Which doesn't make sense. We hate each other.

"Whaaaaat? Oh, damn!" Asher shakes his head.

"I know," I go on, like I always do. I'm their alpha—the aggressive super star of the school. The guy who crushes anyone who doesn't pay total and complete respect. "Perfect fucking tits. But she saw me. And you know what the Ice Queen had the audacity to do?"

"What?" Asher's upper lip curls. He's the wild one in our school pack. The guy who's usually breaking pack code and getting busted on by the alpha. Like father, like son, I guess.

"She told me to *shoo*." I leave out the way her breasts bounced when she made the motion. What it did to me.

"Oh, shit." J.J. grimaces over the human's audacity at insulting an alpha wolf. "What did you do?"

I paste a shit-eating grin on my face. "I scared the crap out of her."

My wolf doesn't like that, though. I sense a restless disapproval ripple beneath my skin. But I don't know what his problem is. My wolf can*not* want to mate with a human.

And even if he did, it won't happen. It can't.

As it is, there's a 50-50 chance I'll pass my defect on to my pups. If I mated with a human, they would be further degraded, if they even transition to be shifters. Which is why I have to mate with an alpha female.

My dad has drilled this fact into my head since the early months of my transition at puberty when we discovered the family defect presented in me.

He wants me to trick an alpha female into mating me. I might just not mate at all. Avoid passing this shit on to any pups at all.

I remember how he sat beside me on the bed after I passed out—the only time anyone in our family actually needed his skills as a doctor. *It's a genetic anomaly. Your brain's interpretation of ocular input gets mixed up. Basically, your brain is trying to see with your wolf eyes while you're in human form. It's manageable, but you have to hide it. Stay away from fluorescent lights, which can trigger the episodes. When they happen, hide them. You'll have to learn to fake it. Do not tell a single soul about this. No one can know you're not perfect, Abe. You'll have to work to become the alpha of your class and maintain your position, so you secure the best possible mate before it gets worse or anyone finds out.*

Which means for me, there's no chance of me finding my fated mate.

Asher growls approval over me scaring Lauren.

J. J. rolls his eyes. "You're lucky Alpha Green didn't tear a piece out of you."

He means literally. With his teeth. Pack discipline is almost always physical since we heal instantly. It's a show of dominance and a demand for respect.

"He was already dressed," I explain.

"You're fucking lucky," Markley says. "No consequences at all?"

"I told him she was naked, and he chalked it up to raging teen hormones."

"Genius, dude." Sebs offers his knuckles, and I fist-bump him.

"Wait, wait, wait. Let's go back to the naked part," Markley says. "Like full-on naked? Or panties-and-bra naked?"

The other guys snicker and lean their heads in, all waiting for my answer.

Funny, but I wish I'd kept my mouth shut. I offered up the situation to Alpha Green to get him off my back, but now I don't like everyone talking about her tits.

Lauren may be a stuck-up rich girl who doesn't belong in Wolf Ridge, but she doesn't deserve to be disrespected this way. Not even to preserve my reputation as alpha.

"Drop it, Markley," I growl.

"So she wasn't actually naked?" he asks.

"What were you doing at her place, anyway?" Sebs wants to know. "I thought you were chasing Casey and River."

Casey is the female alpha of the senior class. The female I *should* be chasing.

The one I have absolutely no interest in. A mutual feeling, I suspect.

"I was, but I saw lights on at the Sterling mansion, so I went to look."

I don't tell them that I find myself running out to Moongaze Hill every few nights. Sniffing around the place, my wolf inexplicably drawn to that monstrosity of a mansion.

J.J. and Sebs exchange another look.

"What?" Irritation spikes.

Sebs shrugs. "Nothing. She's hot. I'd go look, too."

My wolf snarls, and I turn on him. "You stay away from her."

He raises his brows.

Markley interrupts. "I gotta go or my mom will freak." He fistbumps me and swings the door open to get out.

"See ya."

It's a school night and Sebs is probably the only one who's even looked at his homework. He's the kind of guy who seems to have it all done before I've even cracked a book. Not that we crack books anymore. Wolf Ridge High finally caught up with the twenty-first century this year and provided electronic copies of textbooks.

Which makes it even harder for me. The light from any kind of electronic device fucks with my vision. I'm learning to read using peripheral vision, but it usually takes so much concentration that I don't actually absorb what I'm reading.

I drop off the other guys and pull into my driveway. The back of my neck itches in warning as I climb out of the Land Rover.

Yep. As I feared.

My dad waited up to give me hell.

His biggest fear for me is that I'll mate a human.

Chapter Two

auren
Every time I set foot on the Wolf Ridge High campus, I'm quite sure I'm on the set of a zombie apocalypse movie.

Then again, that might be a projection on my part.

I've been flat-lining for 51 and a half weeks now.

I haven't made a single friend in the month I've been here. I haven't tried. I really can't be bothered when there's no one even worth talking to.

I eat lunch with Lincoln in the cafeteria, but today he's with Rayne, the only girl at this school who is even semi-pleasant. Lincoln has been helping her with math because he is semi-genius level with numbers. He takes after our dad in that area.

I join the two of them, aware we're garnering even more stares than usual. Like Rayne eating with us is worth even more observation than the twins from New York. I seriously don't get this school.

It's so fucking weird.

Rayne confirmed my suspicion that popularity is based

entirely on athletic ability, which explains why Abe Oakley, my asshole chemistry partner, is able to rule the school. He doesn't have that lanky height Lincoln and Luke have at eighteen—the frame that won't fill out until college.

He and his football buddies already look like they're in the NFL. They are huge and ripped.

Even the girls are ripped here. Not Rayne, but she's not a jock or cheerleader like the rest of them. I suspect she's a total outcast, like me and Lincoln.

Hence, the looks.

My gaze unwillingly snags on Abe and his buddies at the table behind Lincoln. He's laughing and saying something to his friends. He gestures, making his biceps jump and bulge.

Muscles that big can't be natural on a guy our age.

I'm wondering if there's a steroid problem here. Some schools struggle with ecstasy. Some with pot. Maybe this one has a real steroid crisis. It would explain the level of aggression and meanness here. Maybe everyone has 'roid rage.

Oh, damn.

Abe looks up and locks gazes with me. His eyes narrow. His dislike for me is obvious. I can't decide if it's because I haven't thrown myself at his feet like the rest of the girls in this school or because I come from money, and this town is working class.

Honestly, I'm not used to being treated like dog shit on someone's shoe, which is how Abe acts, but I don't care.

Making friends here was never a priority.

Now that our gazes have tangled, I refuse to look away. I may not care about ingratiating myself to him, but that doesn't mean I'm going to take any of the crap he throws my way, either.

I purse my lips and stare back, like I just ate something sour.

Abe gets up, and it's like he's the king on a throne the way his buddies instantly stand with him. He swaggers in my direction.

"Oh great," Rayne mutters and ducks her head like she's bracing for a beat-down.

Lincoln and I aren't ruffled. Maybe they all hate us because we think we're better than them, but I guess when it comes to this shit—we are.

Neither of us will ever be intimidated by school bullies. We were the popular kids at Landhower Prep. We're not about to go down on bended knee to worship these losers.

Abe and two of his friends sit down at our table. He pretends the focus of his interest is Rayne, but I know he's here to get a rise out of me. "Look at that. The runt finally made another friend."

It's a shame he's so good-looking. It makes it hard to look away.

"Two," his friend J.J. says, looking between me and Lincoln. "Or do two losers only add up to one?"

Abe slides right up against me, invading my space. I send him my best back-off look, but he only smiles. His teeth are white and perfect, lips far too sensual to belong to such a manly-man. "I didn't think Pearls would lower herself to make friends in Wolf Ridge."

Pearls. That's what he calls me because we're rich. He's always making comments about our mansion and the car we drive.

"I'll bet they go to Homecoming as a threesome. That would be cute, right?" The other guy, Markley, says.

The smile vanishes from Abe's face. In fact, he suddenly looks downright dangerous. Prickles of warning stand out on my arms, but I can't figure out what I should be afraid of.

"As long as we're all there to watch you get crowned king, right?" Rayne tosses back.

His grin returns.

Right. Abe will be Homecoming king. I wonder who his queen will be? Not that I care. I have no plans to go to the dance.

"Pass," I say. Spending more time with the kids from this school would be nothing but painful.

That flash of irritation crosses Abe's face again, but he recovers quickly, pasting his shit-eating grin back on. "You know what would be funny?"

"What?" J.J. asks.

"To put these three losers on the ballot."

"Why?" Markley asks.

I don't get it. Unless...he really *does* want me there to see him get crowned.

Maybe the big-shot bully is actually interested in me.

Ha.

That's hilarious.

"Make it happen," he says to his buddies like he's the movie star, and they are all his personal assistants.

"You know what would be even funnier?" Rayne gives him a saccharine smile. "Watching you lose to an outsider."

That would be funny. My brother is definitely Homecoming king material. He's not a jock, like the assholes at this school, but he's got his rock-boy vibe going on. He's tall, laid-back and very good-looking. Back at Landhower when he smiled, girls swooned.

"In your dreams, Runt." Abe's swagger is firmly in place. He gets up and walks away, his entourage following.

"That was literally the dumbest interaction I've ever

had the misfortune of witnessing. How are these idiots popular?" I ask, trying not to stare at Abe's muscled shoulders as he walks away.

"No idea," Rayne mutters.

* * *

Abe

I hate Chemistry.

The fluorescent lights in the lab trigger my defect, so I can never read what she writes on the board.

And worst of all?

The ice queen is my lab partner, constantly distracting me with that apple candy scent of hers.

I glance over. Nothing about her seems to indicate last night's interlude affected her. She looks well-rested. Hot as hell. Ripe with confidence.

My idea of putting her on the ballot for Homecoming was half-baked. Do I actually want her to be my queen? That's ridiculous.

I know I should dial back on picking on Rayne the Runt—another defective wolf. The shifter who can't shift. If anyone should understand defects not being a choice it's me. You'd think I'd grow out of this petty bully shit and cut the girl a little slack, but every time I see her it's like I can't control myself. She represents everything I hate about myself. The little stab of guilt I've always felt shitting on Rayne becomes a tidal wave when I see the disgust on Lauren's face. I push it down.

I refuse to let this snobby weak human make me feel guilty. I'm alpha here. She may not get what that means, but she will. Even if that means putting her in place myself.

She won't be voted queen. Casey Muchmore will win

queen. She's the female alpha of the school. My dad has already asked me four times if I've asked her to the dance.

Of course, I should.

Is it strange I've never been interested in her?

When I first transitioned and discovered I had a flaw, my dad started pushing hard on the female alpha thing. So I dated cheerleaders and volleyball stars. I fooled around with the bolder she-wolves on full moon runs. And then Lauren Sterling showed up, and my stupid wolf got a hard-on for her.

A beautiful, snobby human.

She tosses her long auburn waves over her shoulder and gives me a cool, disaffected look as we stand at our lab counter.

Anyone else—any shifter kid in this class—would've done the work for me. They would've groveled and simpered and given me any information I needed to somehow get a C in this class, so I could stay on the football field.

I am the alpha at Wolf Ridge High, after all.

I can manipulate all with a single look. A lift of my brow. The wave of my hand.

No one would even think to question why I need the help. They assume I'm just demanding their loyalty and service.

But not Lauren.

And this spoiled princess is completely unaffected by my power and status at this school.

Ms. Miller passes out the lab instructions. Lauren ignores me and slips a pair of goggles over her head that magnify her teal blue eyes. Normally, big eyes make a female look innocent. Fragile. Sweet.

Not this princess.

The haughtiness she exudes cancels all cuteness from

her appearance. Still, she somehow manages to look runway-model hot in plastic eyewear.

I put my goggles on the top of my head like I'm too cool to wear them. Which is true.

Miller won't call me on it, either. There's no point in me wearing them. Shifters can't be hurt by chemical burns. Well, temporarily, sure. But nothing that wouldn't heal overnight.

I lean a hip against the lab counter and fold my arms across my chest to watch Lauren work.

She sends a glare my way. "You're not even going to pretend to help?"

My wolf is satisfied she finally addressed me. Finally looked my way. "Nope."

The students on the other side of our lab bench—both shifters—give me the obligatory chuckle.

I'm their king, entertaining.

Lauren ignores them. "You don't think Ms. Miller will notice?" she asks coolly. She's always unruffled by my attempts to engage her. It drives my wolf fucking bonkers.

Or maybe that's my ego.

"Miller's not going to do anything," I say with total confidence. I'm not as certain as I sound, but my dad *is* pack royalty, and Miller's just a school teacher. Nobody special. She would know that if I fail this lab, my grade will slip below a C, and I won't be able to play in the game this weekend. That would bring a ton of pressure on her from nearly everyone in the town, from Coach Jamison and the principal to every ordinary citizen who depends on Wolf Ridge High to be their weekly entertainment.

Lauren's nostrils flare, and her lips turn down in an expression of distaste as she moves with confidence, measuring dried peas and sand in two separate beakers. I'm familiar with this particular look–it's pretty much the only one she gives me.

She shakes her head as she works. "I hear you have the possibility of a football scholarship. How's it going to work in college when you won't have the first clue how to get through a class without bullying someone else to do your work?"

I'm satisfied she knows things about me, since most of the time she pretends I don't exist, but the mention of college turns my stomach. Especially because her words are way too close to the truth. There's no way I will make it through college without paying or threatening someone to do my work.

I give her my best shit-eating grin. "What makes you think I won't be able to bully someone in college?"

She rolls her eyes. "One of these days, someone is going to take you down, Oakley. And I'm going to laugh my ass off."

Fuck, I love hearing the sound of my name on her lips. Even if it is only my last name.

"Maybe you should try." I don't know what makes me say it. Just that I crave more of a reaction from her. More than the indifferent tosses of that thick, glossy mane. The one I want to use to tug her head back. To make her bare her throat to me, even though she has no idea what submission means.

I want her hands on me, pushing back. Giving it to me the way I crave giving it to her.

She sends me a sidelong glance. "Maybe I will."

She's probably not flirting. Considering her complete disregard for me, that would be a dumb assumption.

But my dick takes it as if she is. It surges against my

zipper, and suddenly I'm dying to know what it would feel like to have those pouty lips wrapped around its girth.

I step closer, crowding against her side. "Oh yeah?" My voice isn't threatening. It's a deep, suggestive rumble. Almost a purr. I lower it even more. "What would you do?"

The kids across the lab counter from us have their heads down. They're shifters, which means they can hear every word, but they're giving us some privacy. Letting Lauren believe they can't hear my murmured words.

Now that I'm in close, her apple scent swirls up in my nostrils, making my dick thicken even more. I want to nibble that neck and find out how she tastes.

Scratch that, I want to pick her up, sit her ass on the lab table, spread those knees, and taste her where it counts most.

She turns her face up and only jerks slightly to find me so close. Her pupils dilate–the first indication I've seen from her that she's attracted to me. That she knows any emotion at all. My wolf nearly snarls out loud in victory.

If she were scared right now, her pupils would narrow, and I would smell fear on her. Our faces are inches apart, and she doesn't step back. I detect cinnamon on her breath from the gum she tossed away when she walked into the room.

To my delight, she lifts her chin and leans in closer, almost like she's going to kiss me. Or more likely, bite me. She probably wants to, considering what a dick I've been. "If I told you," she purrs with the same suggestive tone, "you'd be prepared for it." She pulls away enough to see my entire face. "And I want it to hurt." Her eyes gleam like the thought of giving me pain turns her on.

Before I can think, I've looped an arm around her back and yanked her soft body right up against mine.

The moment my brain comes back online, I expect her to fight like a wildcat. She doesn't. She stiffens but remains in place, quickly hiding the startled expression on her far-too-perfect face. I swear I catch the scent of female arousal.

My wolf roars to life beneath my skin. Suddenly the urge to shift is overwhelming–almost like it was at the height of puberty when I couldn't control it.

"Let go of me, asshole," she murmurs, but her voice doesn't match the words. She's breathless, and there's no anger behind the murmured syllables.

Ms. Miller, noticing the interaction, strides over to the lab desk, and I reluctantly ease my hold on the delectable human.

"Is there a problem over here?" I catch the warning in my teacher's look: *Don't mess with humans.*

It's Lauren who answers, though. "No," she chirps, seemingly recovered from our interlude. "Abe's just giving me moral support while I do the lab."

It's an obvious challenge to Ms. Miller, who can't possibly fail to respond.

"Abe, you will help your lab partner by sharing the work." There's more of an entreaty than a warning in our teacher's voice.

I nod and slip my lab goggles over my eyes. "Of course, Ms. Miller. I'm here to learn."

She and I both know it's not true, but she accepts it. "Good." She walks away, and the kids across the lab desk snicker softly.

I ignore them, still turned on by the haughty little human who thinks she can bring me down. I let my hand slide lightly across her upper back. "What can I do to help, princess?"

* * *

Lauren

My heart thunders against my chest.

It's the first time I've felt anything in ages.

The feeling is hate.

I hate Abe Oakley.

I mean, I hate this whole school, but Abe Oakley embodies everything that's backward and wrong about this place.

I should be back in Manhattan with the rest of the Suntan Six—my friends from Landhower Prep school. The ones I go to St. Bart's with every year. The ones who have completely forgotten about me since I moved.

Instead, I'm drowning in this weird-ass fishbowl of a town. The sensation of being underwater is real.

But I guess I had it even before we came here. I had it from the moment my mom was diagnosed with breast cancer.

I just went...*numb*.

I didn't even cry at the funeral. I haven't cried once.

It's fucked up and wrong.

Something is definitely wrong with me.

So actually, the fact that Abe inspires *any* feeling in me is a welcome relief. The effect he has on my body is inexplicable. I'm hot all over, with a slow pulse thrumming between my legs.

I have a boyfriend back in New York. One I need to break things off with because I feel absolutely nothing for him. Even before the situation with my mom—before I lost my ability to feel—Luke never inspired feelings like this in me.

"Light the burner and heat that solution," I order.

To my shock, the jock obeys, but with that cocky grin still firmly in place. Like the only reason he's helping is to get a further rise out of me.

His pompous arrogance somehow manages to pierce the plasma bubble around my body and elicit a response. Annoyance, mostly.

But today, a little more.

I do care about my dad. Lincoln and I are here for him. After almost losing him, too, we didn't protest when he decided abruptly that we should all go live in the vacation house he built for my mom in Arizona.

We didn't opt to go to Cave Hills—a much better school that's farther away because we wanted to stay close to monitor his mental health.

"Now what, partner?" Abe stands too close. I wish he wasn't such a perfect specimen of manhood. Not that I'm into jock-types. Not at all.

But It's hard to ignore Abe's sheer masculine virility when he's right beside me. He's a foot taller than I am and probably weighs twice as much because his body is built of solid muscle.

Solid.

Muscle.

I know because I just felt the hard-as-rock relief of his chest when my hands flew up against it to push him back. I may have memorized the ridges of his washboard abs.

I would like to say I never craved tracing the exquisite lines of his upper arms. That I haven't wondered whether he has a six-pack or eight-pack. It's not about how you work out, it's genetic—I learned that last year in AP biology.

That's the only reason I return the favor of touching his back. I pat it like a child and give him my most condescending, "Good job, Abe" when he brings the solution to a boil.

I expect another lazy smirk, but his upper lip curls in a snarl that makes me snatch my hand away. It was an instinctual reaction. I'm not afraid of him, but something about that look startled me.

Like most bullies, he usually plays offense. He's the one poking at others.

I blink, and it's gone. The smile doesn't return, but Abe's face goes somewhat blank.

I'm not sure how to interpret that reaction. Abe's insecure about his intelligence, maybe?

I decide to go back to ignoring him and doing the lab on my own.

"You're good at this," he says after I'm the first one finished, and Ms. Miller comes over to praise us.

It's not hard. It's not even an AP class–they don't have one here. So I shrug. "I guess."

"You're going to help me study for the test," he declares.

I shake my head. "In your dreams, baller. I have better things to do than teach your sorry ass about chemistry."

The pirate smile is there. Good thing I'm immune to it.

Good thing I have a boyfriend.

The one I'm breaking up with.

"You'll do it. I just have to find your leverage point. Everyone has one. So what's yours?"

But, that's the thing–I don't have one. I'm a teenager who just lost her mom. Nothing else could hurt at this point. Nothing even touches me. I truly have no fucks to give about anything other than keeping our dad alive.

Abe considers me. "Pleasure?" His grey eyes sweep up and down my body with...is it appreciation? Heat? It's the first time I've seen anything other than cockiness or scorn on that beautiful face of his. "Or pain?"

I don't know why his words hit me physically. And

when I say physically, I mean, well, *sexually*. My core tightens, and my nipples get stiff. Parts of me I didn't even know existed rev to life.

Abe's nostrils flare, and he steps a little closer. "Hmm? Which is it?" His voice is a low rumble. Like honey over coffee grounds. "Or is it both together?" There's innuendo in his tone. A leer in his expression.

Oh, God. It does nothing to quiet the stirring between my legs.

I'm not attracted to him. Abe's about as far from my type as a guy could be. But for some reason, my body is all lit up. My belly squirms. Heat prickles across my skin.

I've never felt this way about Luke—even before I went numb.

Maybe it's just that I felt nothing for so long that feeling *anything* shocks me, but I have to take a step back.

As nice as it is to know I'm not actually dead, the sensations are too overwhelming.

Abe doesn't give me space, though. He steps in again, closing the gap between us. "Let's try both." He strokes a lock of hair back from my goggles. I shake off his touch, and he grins.

I smile back. A saccharine smile in which I try to convey all the hatred I have for the school, this town, and Abe. "Touch me again, and I will take you down, Abe Oakley," I say in a soft suggestive tone.

For a moment, I swear his grey eyes take on a strange glow. They get lighter—almost ice blue.

I'm not afraid of him, but it sends a shiver down my spine.

To cover it, I push away from the chemistry lab desk, grab the hall pass by the door, and flounce out of the room.

I feel that laser beam gaze on my back the entire time,

even after I've disappeared from his sight. Once I can breathe freely again, I consider why it is I don't tell Abe that I have a boyfriend. If this is his pathetic attempt at flirting, that knowledge should make him back the hell off.

I'm not keeping options open for when I break up with Luke–the task I've been putting off for weeks.

It's not because of those washboard abs or broad shoulders. That pirate smile.

It's definitely not because I enjoy his attention.

It's probably just that he doesn't deserve that much personal knowledge about me.

Yeah, we'll go with that.

Chapter Three

be

The scent of the human's arousal makes me feverish.

The ice princess isn't frigid.

I scented her arousal in class today when I suggested giving her pleasure. Or was it the promise of pain?

Hard to say what brought about her reaction; all I know is that it both satisfied my wolf and increased my need to dominate her.

Which is why I can barely contain my wolf during football practice. I need to shift and run off this crazy energy.

"Oakley!" Coach Jamison bellows when I catch the ball and plow down the field knocking my teammates out of the way. When I cross into the end zone, I jump ten feet in the air to spike the ball.

"Cool it, Abe," Coach Jamison growls. We're not supposed to show our superhuman strength at school or during any game. But I can't fucking help it. Ice Princess is under my skin.

Which makes me need to get under her skin. I'm dying to figure out where her pain points are. What makes her haughty facade crumble.

I want to hurt her. The way her body responded when I mentioned the combination of pleasure and pain has my mind going down a perverse road now.

My teammates, catching my energy level and responding to their alpha, hurtle themselves my way, attempting to dogpile me.

Bodies fly through the air knocking into me. I knock and throw them off, but the whole team works together, and soon I'm on my back, pinned by a dozen laughing packmates.

Boys will be boys, as they say. Male wolf aggression has to be let out in some way. Especially in high school when hormones and females drive us mad.

"Oakley."

It's Wilde, my older brother's best friend, and our new assistant coach. He's two years older than I am. I respond to his authority more than Coach's, for some reason. Maybe because my brother is like a god in our household, so Wilde, by association, represents what I'm supposed to aspire to.

I'll never live up to Austin with his perfect grades and academic scholarship to ASU, but Wilde's even bigger. He got a full football scholarship to Duke, but he's back home because he fucked up, and that's why he's here helping coach the team at the moment.

Coach Jamison and Alpha Green all think I might be able to do even better than Wilde. Of course, my dad wants me to play in-state, so he can monitor my condition in case it gets worse. I'll be right back to living in Austin's shadow there, the kid brother with the defect he has to hide from the pack.

But maybe the ice princess was right—I wouldn't be able to fake it in college without pack members around to manipulate. My defect would become my undoing—especially if I went to an academically rigorous school.

Wilde yanks me to my feet and bares his teeth. "Stop fucking around, Oakley. You know better."

I give him my lazy grin, but he's not looking. His head whips around, and even with my defect, I can see what he's looking at.

Rayne the Runt—Wilde's new stepsister—is walking along the fence with the ice princess and her twin.

My dick twitches at the sight of Lauren's shapely legs. All that golden skin showing. She's in a short pink skirt and a top that criss crosses her breasts, showing skin at the sides of her waist. Even though I can't see clearly from here, I remember every fucking detail of exactly how hot she looks in that outfit from Chemistry today.

A low growl sounds in Wilde's throat, and his nostrils flare.

I force myself to stop staring at the ice princess. I can't let anyone think I'm attracted to a human. I have my position as alpha of my class to protect.

"The runt has a thing for humans, doesn't she?" I jeer to distract from the real focus of my attention.

Wilde's body goes rigid, his gaze still pinned to the threesome. "Shut the fuck up, Oakley," he snarls.

Yeah, I don't know why I imagined we'd bond. Of course, he's not going to confide in me how he feels about suddenly having the pack runt become a member of his family, not to mention his current suspension from Duke's football team while he's being investigated on drug charges.

He may be best friends with Austin—I may have grown

up with him practically living at my house–but that doesn't mean we share a bond.

The three walk to the Wonder Twins' Tesla S and climb in.

"They don't belong here," I observe–as if that's what bothers me.

It's a bandwagon I can lead–marginalizing the two rich kids who think they own the world showing up at our school and completely ignoring the social order. They think they're special because they play music and live in the mansion on the hill and drive an electric car when in actuality, they're the lowest of the low in this town.

Humans.

Basic. Fragile. Nothing.

I should be all over Casey Muchmore, the alpha she-wolf of the senior class. My wolf should want to breed her to preserve the best genes. Instead, he's after a girl I can't have.

And with my defect, I need the most optimal female in the pack as my mate.

As the car pulls away, Pearls rolls down the window, and her dark auburn hair blows back. I can't see her face, but I would swear she's looking my way.

Maybe thinking about my threat.

Wondering how I will deliver the pain. And the pleasure.

I know exactly the way I want her–on her knees. Face turned up, mouth open for my cock.

I want her sorry for ever coming here.

Sorry for not dropping to her knees for me sooner.

I want her...fuck it, yeah. I want her on her back, thighs open, head back, screaming my name. I want her needy and wet and squirming beneath me for more. I want to be the guy–the only guy–who gives her pleasure. Make sure she knows who masters her body and who she needs to suck up to if she wants more.

Wilde finally turns and gives me a shove. "Move it, Oakley."

I give my head a shake to fling away the images of Lauren that crowd my mind. What am I even thinking?

She's a human, and I'm the alpha of this school. I shouldn't even give the ice princess the time of day.

Not even to prove I'm her king.

* * *

Lauren

"Hi, Dad."

When we get home from school, I find my dad as I always do–in his office, staring out the window at nothing.

I go in and kiss him on the cheek. "How was your day?"

When he turns, there's so much misery in his expression that if I weren't so numb, it would slay me. My dad has aged twenty years in appearance since my mom first started chemo two years ago.

He drips grief and depression.

Barely functions. Cries at the drop of a hat.

"Did you eat the lunch I left you?"

"Yeah. Thanks, honey."

I can tell he's lying. He usually eats two bites and throws the rest out. It's hard to get him through the basics of life–eating, showering, working.

We're lucky he was financially successful before our mom's illness, or we'd be fucked right now. I don't think he does anything all day.

Friday is the anniversary of my mom's death. It's hard to believe it's been an entire year since she took her last breath.

It's hard to believe how much pain still surrounds our family. Moving to Arizona to feel closer to her certainly didn't fix anything. All it did was isolate us from our friends. Make us even more lonely.

But I get that my dad needed a change. He believes he'll find my mom's energy here. She was the one who loved Wolf Ridge. She was always drawn to the Arizona outdoors for some reason completely unfathomable to the rest of the family.

"I bought a gun."

My heart stops. *"What?"*

We suspect my dad attempted suicide after our mom's death. There was an "accident" with sleeping pills and Scotch that resulted in him getting his stomach pumped. When he got out of the hospital, we made the plan to move here.

My dad waves toward the corner where I see a shotgun propped on end. "For that rabid wolf that tried to attack you. Fish and Game haven't put it down. I'm going to shoot the damn thing, myself."

"Dad, Fish and Game can handle it." I don't like the idea of my dad having a gun.

At all.

My phone rings.

"Go on," my dad says. "That will be Luke."

Luke.

The boyfriend I need to break up with. Today. Today is the day.

It has nothing to do with Abe making me feel something in chemistry class. This should have happened before I even moved here.

He calls every day at this time–I don't even know why. It's not like he misses me. I can tell from his Insta and all the one-sided conversations that his social life is full and rich. I think he's just staying with me because it boosts his reputation. I was the queen at Landhower. Maybe he thinks I'm coming back. I don't know.

Even though we talk every other day, I can't remember if I ever really cared about him. It seems like we were just together because we were supposed to be. Because I was popular, and so was he. We're both good-looking. We run in the same circles. Good enough, right?

When my mom got sick, I lost interest in everything, including him, but he didn't seem to mind.

I swipe my thumb across the screen to answer as I turn to walk out of my dad's office. "Hey, Luke." I head into my bedroom and flop down on my bed.

Our conversations have gotten shorter and shorter. I literally have nothing to say to this guy. I can't even call up the image of his face in my mind.

"What's going on?" he asks.

"Another day in the desert." My voice is as dry as the dust outside.

"Yeah?" he says as if I actually said something interesting. "We ditched today. Everyone ducked out at lunch and went downtown to see the new MOMA exhibit."

I guarantee no one at Landhower actually cares about seeing the MOMA exhibit. They're just about doing what's trendy and expensive.

"What was it?"

"What do you mean?" Luke proves my point.

"What was the exhibit?"

"Oh, I don't know–I hung out in the cafe with Breon

and Tahlia. Did you talk to Lincoln about coming here for Homecoming?"

Fuck. This again.

"Luke, I told you I can't. My dad still isn't doing well."

"Lincoln will be there to take care of him. You have to come—I got a new Armani suit, and it's going to look sick with you on my arm."

Luke's insistence doesn't pierce my thick layer of emotional indifference.

I suspect it's that very thing that keeps him interested in me. Like the fact that I don't care about him or us makes him believe I'm even more special. Even more worth keeping.

When, in fact, the opposite is true.

I have absolutely nothing for this guy. I'm an empty shell.

"Listen, I'm not coming. I think we should break up."

"What? Why? I thought you said there was no one even worth your time in Scottsdale."

"Wolf Ridge." This guy can't even remember the name of the town I live in. "There isn't. But there's no point in you and me staying together. You should ask someone else to the dance."

"Well, I will. But let's not break up, yet. I'll come out there for your Homecoming, and we can talk it over."

I think of Abe and his insistence on putting me on the Homecoming ballot. I do not understand why everyone is so obsessed with this stupid dance.

"I'm not going to the Homecoming here."

"I already told everyone we were going together. And I bought the suit."

Christ. He seriously can't hear me.

"We're not going. I don't want to do this."

"Lauren, we've been together for eighteen months. The least you can do is have the courtesy of breaking up with me in person."

Oof. That's probably legit. I know I've become a zombie in all my relationships. I do owe Luke more than what I've been giving. That's what he insisted when we started having sex.

My mom was in the middle of chemo, and my dad was a mess. Luke said I was checked out. He said real human connection–through sex–would fix it.

I figured I was going to lose the V-card sooner or later. I thought he might be right. I went through the motions for him, but it meant nothing to me. I see now that I was already losing my ability to feel at that point.

Which is what makes Abe's effect on me today all the more unusual.

I give a big sigh. "Fine. It's a week from Saturday. Let me know your travel plans, and I'll pick you up at the airport."

"Cool."

"Okay, I gotta go to the library to study. I'll talk to you later, then."

"All right. Tell Lincoln and your dad I said hi."

He says it every time. I don't bother passing the message. "Yep. Bye, Luke."

"Bye, love."

I end the call and wrinkle my nose. I hate the whole plan. But it's not like I have to have sex with Luke when he comes. Or that I wanted to go to the dance with someone else.

He's coming, so I can break up with him in person. I can learn what it's like to have closure–something I can't seem to find with my mom's death.

I walk to the window and look out. The sun is setting, casting a pink hue on the rocky mountainside. I lean my forehead against the windowpane. A bird startles from one of the trees, and I look over.

There, sitting on his haunches at the edge of our property is the silver wolf. The same damn wolf that nearly ripped out my throat last night.

Chapter Four

Abe

Lauren is absent Friday which annoys the crap out of me.

Is she sick? Humans are so fucking fragile. Her twin is also absent. They could both be sick. Or maybe they went on a trip. Whatever the reason, it makes me want to tear the chem lab apart.

I'd like to say it's only because I need her to get through this damn lab. If I don't get a passing grade for the week, I don't get to play football in tomorrow's game, and Coach Jamison and my dad will straight-up murder me.

But the truth is that I don't even care about the lab. My wolf is restless to see her. I need to fill my nostrils with her candy apple and cinnamon scent. He's howling at the thought that she may be sick.

Like he's going to rush over to the Sterling mansion and somehow save her.

The flicker of fluorescent lights in the chem lab brings on a stabbing pain in my temples. I scan the lab information sheet that Ms. Miller passed out, willing it to come into focus. To make sense. But my gaze can't track the words from my periphery. I see the letters, but they're jumbled.

Fuck.

I think of Lauren again, and my vision becomes chaotic—a dark blur everywhere but the edges.

I give my head a hard shake.

Chemistry lab.

I have to pass this, or I can't play in tomorrow's game.

I glance at the pair of students on the other side of the lab table. They are pack members. They would help me out if I asked.

But that would show weakness. They would wonder why I don't know what's going on.

We decided back in eighth grade I would never let anyone in this pack find out my weakness. My dad didn't want any blemish in our family line to get out.

So I move mechanically, setting out the equipment the kids on the other side of the table are setting out, copying their movements.

Then I realize the answer. It's the tactic I always use when I have to cover my weakness.

Assholery.

"Hey, Newt." I jerk my head at the kid on the other side of the lab table. "You're my partner today. Come over here and run this for me."

His neck gets red—whether it's from anger or just attention from his alpha king isn't clear. Either way, he does what he's told and comes around the table to take over.

I lean against the lab table and pull out my phone, pretending to scroll, even though I can't see a fucking thing at the moment.

Damn that Lauren Sterling.

She's making my defect worse. And now I don't know

how I'll get through the hours until the end of practice when I can shift and stalk her again. Find out what in the hell is so wrong that she had to miss a day of school and fuck me over like this.

* * *

Lauren

The trouble with having a twin is that they're always up in your business.

Especially today–the anniversary of our mom's death.

We're all feeling like fragile freaking flowers in the Sterling household on account of the date. Lincoln and I both stayed home from school in a show of solidarity with our dad. Now that I've been inside all day doing absolutely nothing, I'm regretting that choice.

I don't want to announce that I need time alone, though. It feels selfish.

Lincoln and my dad would both worry about me if I did.

So, after dinner, I slip out the back door without saying anything to either of them, hoping it takes Lincoln longer than ten minutes to realize I'm gone.

Our new house is gigantic compared to what we had back in New York. It's a mansion built into the side of a foothill. I'm still not used to the terrain. The browns and tans. The rocks and dust. The sauna-like Arizona heat.

It's September, and the days are still in three digits. I guess global warming has hit Arizona with a vengeance. I can't take much more. I unbutton and tie the bottom edges of my short-sleeved linen shirt into a knot at my belly.

I walk up the side of the mountain, not following any

path. The yucca scrapes my calves. Dirt and gravel slip into my Vans, which I, unfortunately, am wearing without socks.

The sun is just starting to set, bathing the mountainside in hues of orange and yellow. The white spines on the cacti take on an iridescent glow.

When I get to the crest of the hill, I look down at the house, then at Wolf Ridge beyond it.

Weird freaking town.

But Wolf Ridge and its unfriendly inhabitants aren't worth my thoughts tonight.

I hike across the mesa, so I can keep climbing up. I'm not a hiker–not like our mom. I don't normally head out to commune with the saguaros at sunset.

But she did. She loved Arizona because her mother did. Something to do with a formative trip to the Grand Canyon after my grandmother graduated from Sarah Lawrence. And so today, I'm going to try to find the magic they both felt here.

I'm desperate to connect with my mom. To feel something. Anything—grief. Mourning. Loneliness. Something beyond the numbness.

I climb the ridge. There's no trail to follow. I should probably be afraid of getting lost out here, but I'm not. I guess I'm tempting fate right now.

Give me something to fear.

Make it real.

Show me I'm still alive and care about living.

It's not that I'm suicidal like my dad.

That would require me to actually care about this life. I don't.

I can't make myself care about anything.

After a half-hour's hike, I come up to a ledge where the rock drops 40 feet to a canyon below.

In the trees to my right, I think I catch movement, but when I look, nothing is there. I remember the wolf that tried to attack me through my window. I've had this feeling for weeks that there's something there. Like I'm being stalked.

My dad is afraid the wolf is rabid. He keeps calling the Fish and Game Department asking if they've killed it yet.

A niggling of guilt runs through me. I'm not afraid of a wolf attack, but if something did happen to me out here on the anniversary of Mom's death, it would kill my dad and Lincoln.

I sit cross-legged on the edge and pull out a handwritten letter from my mom. She wrote one for each of us, to help us cope after she died. To remind us that she loved us. I reread her words.

Grieve me together. Support each other. When you three are ready, I'd like you to scatter my ashes in the foothills of our Arizona residence—make that a special, sacred place you can commune with me. The land and light always felt magical to me there. Let it be the place you can find me when you need to connect. But know that no matter where you are, I'll always be with you. Never doubt it.

I do fucking doubt it.

I don't even know if I believe in the afterlife.

And if I did, would I even be worthy of my mom's promise? A daughter who couldn't even cry at her funeral?

I reread her letter, trying to bring something up.

I squeeze my eyes closed. Somewhere, deep beneath the surface, I feel *something*. A disquiet.

I scrunch up my face as if I'm crying, hoping to bring it to the surface. Like maybe if I fake-cry it will come out.

Nothing.

Fuck.

I'm the worst daughter ever.

It sucks to suck, as Lincoln would say.

I stand and peer over the edge of the cliff. This should scare me.

There's no biological response to the threat of death. No uptick in the rate of my pulse or breath. No clammy hands.

I lean over the edge.

Still nothing.

For fuck's sake, what is wrong with me?

I take one foot off the ledge and hold it forward like I'm going to step off a diving board.

In my periphery, I catch a flash of silver. I whirl to find an enormous wolf—the wolf—leaping through the air at me.

I scream as he lands on silent paws in front of me.

My arms pinwheel, but it's too late, the balance of my weight is tipping over the side of the cliff. I'm falling—

Falling—

The wolf's mighty jaws snap and catch on the knot of my shirt.

Great. Instead of smashing to my death below, I'm going to be eaten by a wolf.

But no—my shirt tears.

I buckle in half, reaching for the cliff's edge as my ass plunges below it.

Apparently, I choose being eaten by a wolf over plummeting because my flailing hand reaches for the wolf's nape, fingers closing on fur.

Fingers closing on...

My feet dangle in the air, but I'm not falling.

I'm suspended over the edge of the cliff, hanging by my arm which is held in a vise-like grip by...

Abe Oakley.

Wait...*what?*

A *shirtless* Abe Oakley.

Where did he come from? Did I black out? What in the hell is happening?

And then it all becomes clear.

Because Abe opens his mouth and the torn piece of my shirt flutters from his jaws.

Abe Oakley is a wolf.

He hauls me up over the edge of the cliff, pulling me on top of him, and rolling both of our bodies, so I'm on bottom, and he's on top.

And that's when I realize–

Abe is *completely* naked.

I mean, I guess that makes sense.

The wolf wasn't clothed. And he definitely was–*is*–the wolf.

I blink up at him.

I'm not scared, but it's not because I'm still numb.

On the contrary, for the first time in over a year, I feel *everything*.

The whisper of the hot breeze on my cheeks. The rapid beating of my heart against Abe's chest. A sense of exhilaration. Glory, even.

I didn't die.

I cared about living–I was truly scared there for a moment, but I survived. And it feels *wonderful*.

The sense of being alive. Of having this incredible experience that can't be explained. Of...

Wait. Maybe I did die? I died, and this is like some kind of crazy afterlife dream where my subconscious produced a wolf that turns into Abe Oakley.

"Fuck." Abe's eyes are round, his gaze darting across my face with dawning horror. He rears back. "Fuck, fuck, fuck."

Okay, yeah. This seems real. Abe would do this. But, unlike Abe, he's as freaked out about finding himself naked on top of me as I was about having a wolf trying to bite my midriff.

But no, that's not what happened.

"You saved me," I realize. He didn't bite my flesh, he grabbed my shirt. He was trying to keep me from going over the edge.

Abe scrambles to his feet and stares down at me. His body is more beautiful than Michelangelo's David, his muscles perfectly honed, his very impressive cock standing at half-mast. His throat works. "Yeah. I...saved you from the wolf."

I blink. His voice has the timbre of someone trying out a story. Like he's trying to make me believe he's not the wolf. To help shape an unexplainable situation into something that fits this reality.

Except he's stark naked. And I saw the knot from my shirt drop from his jaws. So, no, I'm not buying what he's selling.

"No, Abe. *You* are the wolf."

* * *

Abe

"Fuck." I wipe my mouth with the back of my hand.

I am so fucked.

I am *beyond* fucked.

This human female is the bane of my existence.

My fear for her—that terror at seeing her step off the

ledge—still pumps through my veins. The only way to save her was to shift back into human form, and now she's seen me.

She knows my secret.

I've broken pack law.

I glare down at her. "What in the hell were you doing?" Adrenaline makes my voice rough. My eyes must be changing color because her lids widen, and her mouth falls open. "You're the wolf who tried to attack me through my window the other night."

"I wasn't attacking you. I—" I try to flip the questions back on her. "Why were you going to jump?"

It's hard to imagine this haughty rich girl is suicidal, but that's what I saw. She literally was stepping off the ledge.

I *had* to do something.

She pushes up to a seated position and tries to smooth the tattered edges of her button-down shirt enough to cover a melon-pink bra. She's unsuccessful. I tore the shirt almost up to her armpits.

I try not to look at the bare skin of her midriff. I'm already out of control enough.

"I wasn't going to jump."

I don't smell a lie on her, but there is a heaviness to her that I didn't notice before. I was too caught off-guard by my reaction to her scent and her body, too annoyed by her haughty demeanor to have realized that she might be unhappy.

But unhappy enough to jump off a cliff? Or to contemplate it? That doesn't seem quite right.

I extend a hand because leaving a female sitting on her ass isn't gentlemanly. I half expect her to slap it away, but she puts her palm in mine.

Out of habit, I modulate my strength to pretend I can't

just lift her weight with total ease, then remember that it's too late for that.

It's too late, and I need to fix this problem fast.

Midway up, I change course, duck my shoulder to fit in the crease of her hip, and lift her straight from the ground to the air.

"Abe!" she shrieks as her torso swings down my back. "What the fuck?"

I'm sure she doesn't appreciate the view of my naked ass or being manhandled this way. I know it's fucked up, but what choice do I have?

I take off running, trying to keep my gait even and smooth, so I don't bounce my upside-down captive too much.

She smacks my bare ass. "Abe! What are you doing? Where are you taking me?"

I don't answer. There's no explaining what's going to happen to her now, and doing so would only traumatize her further. Probably my best bet at this point is to keep my mouth shut until I've fixed this.

What I don't count on—what I never count on—is Lauren stealing my sanity.

She smacks my ass again, then grips one of my buttcheeks and squeezes hard, digging her nails into my flesh. I might have been able to handle the torture of having her hands on my bare flesh if it wasn't for the scent of her arousal blooming right beside my nose.

Before I can even think, a wolf-like snarl leaves my lips, and I turn my head and sink my teeth into her thigh.

Oh fuck!

Fortunately, my canines hit the fabric of her jean shorts, not her actual flesh. I punch holes through the fibers of cotton but stop myself before I puncture her skin.

Oh, fates. *That was a mating bite.*

I just tried to *mark a human.*

A female I don't even know or like.

What is wrong with me? Is my wolf demented?

"What are you doing, Abe?" Lauren kicks her feet, but the scent of her arousal only grows stronger. This girl will be the death of me. It's like she's wired backward, and the worse I treat her, the more turned on she gets.

Maybe she's one of those females who gets turned on by pain or humiliation. By BDSM or whatever they call it.

Humans are so fucking warped.

Except my attempt at scorn barely lasts two seconds before I'm fully on board with giving her whatever she wants. Whatever turns her on. Finding out how to push her buttons in a variety of ways.

I would love to learn how to make Lauren Sterling scream with pleasure. Shriek in pain. Quiver with temptation and need. To torture her the way she's been torturing me since the first day of school.

Of course, I won't. I don't take females non-consensually, not even if they're turned on. Just because her body wants something from me doesn't mean *she* does.

Lauren claws my back, bites my side. Continues to slap my ass. "Let me go, Abe! Put me down!"

I run across the mesa until I get to my family's cabin. Set in the middle of our hunting grounds, it's the place I went after dinner to undress and shift. It's also the haunt my brother and his friends used in high school to bring females for–

No, I can't think of that.

Lauren doesn't want that from me.

"Abe!" There's a note of real alarm in her voice that bothers my wolf.

Bothers him enough to need to soothe her. "Take it easy, princess." I tip her down to drop her to her feet on the porch as I reach for the key above the door frame. "I'm not going to hurt you."

She doesn't run. Maybe she's too shocked by my behavior. I doubt it's because she trusts me or what I just promised. She stares at me as I push open the door to the cabin and step inside to grab my clothes.

"Why did you bring me here?" She follows me to the doorway, standing in the middle of it—neither inside nor out. The pink and purple of the fading sunset make the sky behind her glow, backlighting her with the aura of a goddess.

I don't answer, but yank on a pair of boxers and shorts. I'm thanking the sweet moon she hasn't already taken off running.

It's not because she's turned on by me. It can't be.

She probably craves answers about what just happened. I shifted right before her eyes. *Fuck!*

I had to or she would have plunged to her death below. The thought still makes me sick to my stomach.

But now, I have to do the unthinkable. I have to get her mind wiped.

I shrug on a t-shirt as I walk swiftly to the kitchen to grab duct tape from the junk drawer. "I'm really sorry about this." I advance on her, stretching a length of tape from the roll.

She catches on quickly—she's smart as fuck—I already knew that from chemistry class. In a second, she's bolting out the door, but she's no match for me.

I catch her with just a few long strides and wrap an arm around her waist to haul her off her feet. "Don't freak, princess."

It's hard to describe how satisfying it is to have my mouth pressed against her neck, the silk of her dark, copper hair falling against my jaw. Her apple candy scent gives me a fresh hard-on. "I'm not going to hurt you."

She flails and fights me, her nails digging into my forearm. "You *are* hurting me," she lies.

"I know I'm not. If you'd stop fighting me, I could put you down."

She immediately goes slack. The moment I lower her feet to the ground, she attempts to run again.

I give her ass a smack. "I don't want to do this."

It's only partly true. The satisfaction of picking her up, carrying her to the sofa, and straddling her hips to hold her down is far too delicious to deny. I catch her wrists and hold them together to wind the duct tape around them.

"Wh-what are you doing?"

* * *

Abe

I scent real fear on Lauren now, and it nearly knocks me on my ass. My wolf is going berserk–he wants me to soothe her.

I want to spread her legs and take care of her other needs. The kind that involves her choking out my name on a scream of pleasure.

But neither of those things can happen right now.

I wrap the tape as quickly and efficiently as I can. "Don't freak, Lauren. I mean, of course, you're going to freak because I'm taping your wrists and ankles together, but I swear to fate, I'm not going to hurt you. You just won't remember what happened tonight."

Worst thing to say, apparently.

Lauren loses her shit and headbutts me. It doesn't hurt, but her eyes water, which guts my wolf. I sit her up and crouch at her feet to wrap her ankles together with the tape while she beats me around the head and shoulders with her bound hands.

I finish taping and catch her wrists. "Hey," I say softly, like I'm quieting a spooked horse. "That doesn't hurt me. You're just hurting yourself."

I press her hands down to her lap. "You'll be okay, Pearls. I promise."

I'm not even sure if my promise is true. I mean, what do I know about getting a human's mind wiped? I've never even met a vampire, much less hired one to take care of a mess I made.

If I hadn't already fucked up and been told to stay away from Lauren Sterling, I might risk punishment and take her to the alpha right now. Ask him to clean up my mess and trust that he would do it right.

But that's not an option. Doing so could get me banished from the pack. And banishment for a species like ours would be condemnation to a life not worth living. Just ask Asher, whose dad was banished when he was ten.

I hear a ding from the back pocket of Lauren's jean shorts, and I fish her phone out. It's a text from Lincoln:

Where are you? Are you okay?

Another spike of misgiving runs through me. Why did he ask that? Is she depressed? Suicidal? What is going on with this enigmatic female?

Lauren looks at me, then her eyes widen and she gasps. "The letter!" There's a real panic in her voice. *"Where is the letter?"*

"What letter?"

Her voice raises to a shriek, "Where is the letter I had?"

I try to figure out where her mind is. "The paper? The paper that was in your hand when you tried to jump off the cliff?"

"I didn't *jump* off the cliff! This huge fucking wolf tried to attack me, and I fell." She tries to stand up, teeters, and I catch her before she topples. "I need that letter!"

"I didn't attack you–I tried to keep you from jumping." I search her pockets, ignoring the surge of lust that kicks through me at having my hands all over her hips, but there's nothing there. "You must've dropped it."

"No." She shakes her head vigorously. Her voice sounds strangled "It can't be gone. I'm telling you, Abe, I need that letter! Let me go–I have to find it!"

I stare at her. This night couldn't get any more fucked.

If her scent hadn't turned so metallic, if I couldn't hear the timbre of tears in her voice, I might be able to ignore her pleas. But she's clearly desperate.

"What's in the letter, Pearls? Who is it from?" A ripple of jealousy rolls through me as I consider it might be from a boyfriend back home.

"It's the last letter my mother wrote to me before she died."

I go still.

Oh damn. I had no idea her mom was dead. That's heavy as fuck. I've been such a royal dick to this girl, thinking she was so privileged, and she's suffered a huge loss. Maybe recently. One so much greater than I've ever known. One no teenager should suffer.

Against my better judgment, I make my decision. "Okay, I'll go look for it. But I have to make sure you can't get away."

"What do you mean?"

I pick her up and carry her to the kitchen chair. "Sit here."

"I'm not sure where my choice was in that," she grumbles.

I strap her to the back of the chair with several lengths of duct tape around her middle.

She looks up at me with narrowed eyes. They're teal—the color of the ocean where it froths against rocks. "I hate you, Abe Oakley."

"I'm not your biggest fan either, Pearls," I say. "But that's neither here nor there." I leave her phone by the door where I undress again, my wolf preening when I feel Lauren's gaze on my body. I turn to look over my shoulder and find her attention trained on my ass. She swallows, and I catch the intoxicating scent of her arousal again.

That particular perfume will be the death of me. I angle my hips away from her, so she can't see my dick's enthusiastic reaction.

"Don't move from that spot," I warn, knowing full well she'll probably try everything she can to get free the moment I leave.

"Go fuck yourself."

The practiced alpha in me can't help but pin her with a stare. "Do you want me to go find the letter or not?"

A pretty blush spreads across her cheeks. "Yes," she grumbles.

I cock my head. "Yes, what?"

Her nostrils flare and jaw sets. "Yes, *please.*" The words come out through clenched teeth.

I give her a tight smile. "That's better. Now be good, Pearls, or there will be consequences."

More of that feminine perfume.

She's killing me.

I close the door behind me and shift. I can travel faster on four paws, and I'll be able to scent that piece of paper if it has blown away.

As I run toward the ledge, my mind whirls around what to do. How to handle this.

I need to call my brother, Austin. He might know who I should see, how much it costs, and how it works. From what I've heard, the quicker you intervene and get a memory wiped, the less damage you inflict. Lauren will just need a couple hours erased from her mind. It shouldn't affect that smart brain of hers.

When I get to the ledge, I lower my snout to the earth and sniff. Lauren's scent is all over the place, but I don't smell paper. I peer over the ledge and scan the terrain. I catch sight of something white below. It could be a light-colored rock, but it could be the letter.

Since there's no one around, and I'm in a hurry, I simply leap off the ledge, tucking to roll when I land. It knocks the wind out of me a little bit, but I stand and shake it off. I trot in the location of what I hope is the letter.

It isn't paper. It's the piece of fabric from Lauren's shirt. I pick it up in my mouth, not because she will need it back but because my wolf craves having the hit of her essence in my mouth.

I scan the terrain again, but my eyes don't cooperate. I blink as my vision blurs, and pain shoots across my temples, paralyzes my neck at the base of my skull. I go still to keep from keeling over, breathing deeply.

My wolf whines with the pain.

Fuck.

This is no time for an episode.

My vision goes completely black.

I wait, taking deep breaths to calm my nervous system.

Clear, clear, clear.

My vision will clear.

My dad says when this happens, it's not my eyes, but my brain's interpretation of the signals from my eyes. It's trying to see as a human when I'm in wolf form or vice versa. Was it Lauren's scent that caused it? I release the fabric from my jaws and drop to my belly, pawing at my face to try to rub my temples, praying to Fate this shit will clear up fast.

And that's when the wind shifts. An unexpected scent reaches my nostrils, and I surge back up to all fours.

Where in the fuck is it?

I swing my head from one side to the other, desperately trying to see, to change up the brain signal that's blocked my visual input.

A hard shake of my head, or maybe the massive dose of adrenaline, brings my vision back, and I see what my nose already discovered.

There, thirty feet in front of me, stands a gargantuan grizzly bear.

Not an ordinary bear–a shifter. One clearly out of its territory, not that I could defend ours without my pack.

As if this isn't bad enough, he lifts his snout to the sky and lets out a warbling roar–a warning to me.

And that's when I see it–clutched in the beast's massive, swinging paw–

Lauren's letter.

Chapter Five

be

AThere is no way I will win any battle against a bear. I may be nearly full-sized. I may be alpha of the school, but a lone wolf isn't a match for a grizzly.

Fuck.

Who is he, and what is he doing on our pack land?

Has he gone feral? I note the white around his muzzle. He's an old bear. Maybe bear shifters go senile?

His claws slash through the air in a clear warning, but I can't back down.

Not when he's holding Lauren's letter.

There's only one thing to do–try to appeal to this guy in human form. I shift and stand holding my palms face out.

"Whoa. Take it easy. You're on my pack land, not the other way around. Are you lost?"

The bear doesn't shift, and he doesn't like the question. He lets out a savage bellow. The kind that nearly makes me shift back to wolf form to defend myself. I resist the urge.

"Okay, nevermind. I don't care about that. The thing is– you're holding my girl's letter." I'm not sure what makes me call Lauren *my girl*. I tell myself it's just for simplicity's sake, but my wolf fucking loves it.

"It's from her mom, who died. It means everything to her. She sent me back to get it."

The bear appears to be listening. I don't think he's feral, but he doesn't shift to human form, either. His upper lip is still drawn back showing me his teeth. He swings his head around like he's looking for Lauren.

"She's back in the cabin. I promised I'd get the letter. May I have it? Please?"

I don't expect him to comply. The bear clearly isn't friendly and doesn't care that he's wandered onto wolf territory without permission. He swings his huge paw in an arc. I think it's another threat until I realize he released the letter like he was pitching me a baseball.

I shift and run for it, forgetting to be cautious around him, but he doesn't charge. He stands on two legs, watching me until I've caught the tumbling piece of paper. I carefully take it between my lips, not teeth, so I won't damage it.

The bear wheels around and bounds off at an astonishing speed for such a big and seemingly clumsy animal.

I lower my head and run for the cabin.

I've wasted too much time on this already. I need to get Lauren to a vampire and wipe her memories before this gap of time in her brain becomes too long to explain or too thick with neural connections not to do permanent damage.

* * *

Lauren

The door to the cabin bursts open, and Abe comes barreling through it.

I'm lying on my side, still strapped to the chair, which is

also on its side. I tipped it over in an attempt to get to my phone.

Needless to say, I didn't make it more than a few feet. It was tough going, inch-worming along the floor. I only made it about three feet in the time he was gone.

But, um, *wow*. Here he is. Once more, I'm shocked by his nudity. More shocked by my reaction to it.

Because I suddenly don't know how I ever found Luke attractive.

He's like a little boy compared to Abe.

What would it be like to be underneath all those hard muscles? Or riding on top? A steady pulse starts up between my legs.

But then I catch sight of what's in his hand, and I forget the lusty thoughts pinging around my head.

"You found it."

He stalks through the cabin and slaps the letter down on an end table. There's a grim set to his mouth and tension in those massive shoulders. "I found it."

He turns and takes in my plight. I try not to look below his waist, but it's impossible. And he's...*okay*...wow. Looking ripe and ready. I drag my lower lip through my teeth.

"I see you disobeyed orders."

I forgot how I must look in this ridiculous position. All my weight is on one shoulder, which has now fallen asleep.

"*Disobeyed–*" I sputter. "What, are we in the military?" I can't keep my eyes on his face. My gaze roves all across that perfectly cut body of his, tracing the chiseled edges of every gorgeous muscle. Always coming back to that *one particular* muscle that appears–er–*happy to see me.*

Abe pulls on his boxers and a pair of faded jeans this time and stalks over to me. "You seem to forget who completely controls your fate right now." He picks up the chair—with me in it—and sets it upright as if it weighs five pounds, not over a hundred and twenty-five. I swear his muscles didn't even strain when he did it.

The guy is bionic. He's still shirtless, which means I see every ripple of his huge muscles when he moves. He's beautiful. But such an asshole.

"Yeah, can we go over that piece again?" I send him a baleful look. "What exactly am I doing here?"

"You saw something you shouldn't have. And that's a problem for my pack."

"Your *pack*..." I must've been in shock earlier, or the surrealness of the night kept rational thoughts at bay. But suddenly, I see the big picture.

Why the little town of Wolf Ridge is so weird.

They're all werewolves.

My mouth falls open.

Abe screws his eyes and mouth up. "Fuck!" He paces away from me, pulling a phone out of his pocket and dialing it.

I hear a male voice answer loudly, like he's talking over some kind of gathering or party. "Hey, Bro! What's up?"

"I have a problem. A big one. I need help."

I don't hear the response, but the noise quiets, like the guy on the other end—I don't know if it's a real brother or just a friend he calls *Bro*—goes somewhere private.

"A girl from school saw me shift. A human." I can't hear the other person's responses now, especially when Abe turns his back and walks away, toward what must be a bedroom. "I know, but I can't...Alpha Green already told me to stay away from her. She saw me on the last full moon run, too...Yeah, I fucked up....*No!* She's nothing to me." He sends a dark look over his shoulder.

His words shouldn't bother me. I mean, of course, I'm

nothing to him. He's nothing to me, either. But something about it sticks in my chest. Snags on the sense of abandonment that always opens up like a Grand Canyon-sized crevasse every time I think about my mom.

Maybe that's why I can't grieve her. I'm too busy feeling wounded that she left me. She was supposed to see me grow up. Watch me graduate. Be at my wedding. Explore this mountainside herself at sunset.

The tears that have eluded me well up in my throat, choking me, suffocating me. There's a pressure in my chest so great I swear it will burst. My lower lip trembles.

And then...nothing.

I swallow it back down.

So close.

But how pathetic that it was brought on by self-pity rather than something more altruistic.

I suck.

I return my attention to Abe, who is making "Uh-huh" and other affirmative noises.

"Are you serious?" he asks. "Do you know the combination?" He returns to the living room and shoves the sofa over like it's not a huge, heavy piece of furniture. He flips back the area rug. "Yeah, I see it."

I crane my neck to see what he's looking at. He pulls up a trap door and reaches in, rotating his wrist. The light whir of a dial reaches my ears.

It must be a safe. Sure enough, there's a clicking sound, and he pulls a heavy metal door open.

"Got it." Abe pulls out a neatly wrapped stack of twenties and thumbs through it. "Let me know. Thank you. Don't tell Dad, okay?" So it is his real brother. "Promise? Thanks."

Abe ends the call and pulls a pistol out of the safe. It

looks old-fashioned—like the kind in Wild West movies. A six-shooter, or something.

Alarm bells go off in my head. Is he going to kill me and bury my body out here somewhere?

"What's that for?"

Abe opens the chamber and looks inside then holds his hand out to catch six bullets. When he lifts his head, his eyes seem to glow.

Chapter Six

Lauren

My mind leaps irrationally to *Abe Oakley is going to kill me.*

My body responds with another massive dose of adrenaline, making my heart pound and my legs twitch and strain against the tape around my ankles.

Abe continually provokes actual feels in my body.

I see a trace of amusement on his cocky face. "Relax, Pearls. It's not for you."

"Who's it for?" My voice raises in pitch. "What's your plan, here, Abe?"

He reloads the gun and tucks it in the back waistband of his jeans. He stands and puts on a t-shirt, then counts the money.

His phone rings, and he answers. It must be his brother calling back. After a few short *Okays* and *Got its*, Abe thanks whoever it is and ends the call.

My iPhone beeps with a message. We both look at where it sits on the end table in the turquoise glitter case.

"That will be Lincoln," I tell him in a rush. "He's going

to freak out if I don't come home soon. He's probably already freaking because I didn't answer his last text."

Abe drops the bullets in his pocket and pushes a hand through his hair. He seems different than he is at school. Less sure of himself. Still an asshole but without the derisive edge. This is him without so much swagger.

"Yeah, that's the thing." He looks at me. His eyes are gray blue–a darker version than his wolf's. "It'll be a couple hours–maybe three. So what can you tell him that he would believe?"

I stare at Abe. Does he really think I'm going to help him out here? Why would I? I'm literally the captive.

He seems to read my thoughts because he picks up my mom's letter and stalks toward me. "You want this back?" He raises his brows.

"Give it to me," I snap, tipping the chair forward like I'm lunging at him.

"Think of an excuse. A *good* one."

My mind spins. Twins are great at reading each other without words. "Let me talk to him."

Abe walks over to the stove. He turns on one of the gas burners, and it clicks a few times then flares to life.

I'm still worrying about how to get a message to Lincoln, but all thoughts halt when he holds up the letter from my mom. "Are you thinking, Lauren?"

I lunge against the duct tape as panic floods my veins. "No!"

"Think fast, Lauren. Make it good. Or the letter goes up in flames."

"Tell him I'm at the library!" I shriek. Tears sting my eyes. "Please. Don't burn it."

He doesn't remove the paper from danger. "Is he going to buy it?"

"Yes! I love the library. It's my happy place."

Abe still doesn't move. He considers me, his eyes narrowed.

"I'll help you–I won't try anything. I promise!" I'm speaking fast now, desperate for him to move the paper away from the flame.

He does.

He flicks the burner off and gets the phone. He turns it to my face to unlock it, then squints at the screen.

"Is there something wrong with your eyes?"

I see a tic of irritation around his mouth before his upper lip rises in scorn. "I'm an alpha wolf. We have perfect eyesight."

"*Alpha wolf.*" I turn that over in my mind, more pieces of the puzzle snapping together. The way the kids at school worship him. The way he acts domineering and aggressive. Different from how he is right now.

It's an alpha status thing. A front.

A wolf thing.

Abe lets out a frustrated sound of self-disgust, like he's pissed he showed me more than he meant to again.

The fact is, the more I know about him, the more sense I'm making of this weird, fucked-up town, the less I hate him.

He's the same as any student at Landhower Prep–fronting to stay cool in front of the other kids, trying to stay out of trouble with his parents and other adults.

But I know I am right about his eyes because his jaw flexes, and he blinks several times at the screen before he seems able to even see what he's looking at. He finally gets the text chat open and replies to Lincoln.

"Why is he so worried about you?"

I give Abe a mulish look. "None of your business."

"Why weren't you at school today?" He flicks the letter open and reads the date. "June of last year. When did she die?"

A tidal wave of grief rises up in my chest–so much I feel like my head will explode.

"Was it today?" Abe demands. For some reason, he sounds pissed, but I can't fathom what his problem is.

I drop my head back and stare at the ceiling without seeing anything.

Mom...I need you now.

My vision blurs. Tears stream out of the corners of my eyes.

Finally, It's starting. I'm afraid to say or do anything for fear it will shut off again like it always does.

A sob comes out of my throat.

I squeeze my eyes closed, leaning into the sense of release, of relief, that's coming at letting this out.

Please don't stop. Please keep flowing.

I hardly notice the harsh ripping of tape from my torso.

I'm crying. Another sob fills my lower jaw.

Abe lifts me out of the chair and yanks me against his body. My face presses against his cotton T-shirt. My bound hands are trapped between our bodies.

I'm terrified that this closeness, this interaction will turn the tears off.

Abe Oakley is the last person I feel safe releasing emotion with. Except, that seems to be a lie because with my face hidden in his shirt, it becomes easy to let it go. Soon, my back shakes with sobs, and I soak the front of his shirt with my tears.

Abe doesn't say a word. He doesn't pat my back or make soothing sounds, but he holds me tight, and there's a fierce-ness in the quality of the embrace that matches the intensity of the trapped emotion inside me. It somehow gives me permission to let it all out.

I don't know how long I stand there and cry. It feels like forever and no time at all. All I know is that when I'm done, when the sobs have stopped, and the tears are dry, the emptiness feels like peace.

"I haven't cried." I lift my face from Abe's mascara-smeared shirt and blink up at him.

He uses his thumbs to clean the smudges under my eyes and wipes them off on the tail of his shirt.

"I haven't cried since before she died. Not once. I couldn't get it out. I haven't felt– anything. That's why I was leaning over the edge of a cliff. Not because I wanted to die but because I wondered if I was even capable of feeling fear."

"Were you?"

I shake my head. "No, but then this wolf ran at me and... I don't know, I felt a little something."

Abe gives me an inscrutable look. "I'm sorry, Lauren. Your sucky day is going to keep getting worse. But I swear to fate you'll wake up tomorrow, and you won't remember any of it. And I'll make sure–*motherfucking sure*–that you feel good."

My forehead wrinkles as I try to decode what he's saying. "How?"

Abe doesn't answer, and some of my peace slips away, replaced by a dull sense of dread. There's something wrong here. I'm not afraid of Abe–despite the fact that he's tied me to a chair and is holding me captive. But his plan–whatever it is–feels wrong. Very wrong.

"With drugs?" I ask. "Are you going to drug me?"

His lips close in a firm line. Instead of answering, he scoops under my knees and lifts me up into a honeymoon carry. He drops my phone into the lap of my belly then the stack of cash.

"Sure, I'll hold that for you," I joke dryly.

The corners of Abe's lips turn up briefly as he strides out of the cabin on long legs. His physical prowess is truly mind blowing. He must be three times as strong as an ordinary human. My weight seems to be nothing to him.

And as crazy as all this is—I'm grateful for the distraction. Abe being a wolf and kidnapping me is a powerful interruption to the numbness I've been feeling. It's better than the emptiness that has engulfed me lately.

He carries me out to his vehicle and manages to balance me with one arm as he opens the passenger door. He carefully sits me on the front seat and fastens my seat belt.

"I've seen you before," I realize. Even before the night of the full moon when he was outside my window, I was seeing glimpses of movement from the woods like I did today before he charged on me.

Abe shuts the passenger door without answering, but I know I'm right.

We drive down the hill toward Scottsdale in silence for twenty minutes, and then I start hysterically laughing.

"What?" he demands.

I can't stop laughing—it's that sort of giddy, uncontrollable, slap-happy state. Not funny, but still hysterical. First the tears and now the laughter. Abe seems to ignite all my lost emotions.

"What's so funny?"

"I just realized." I'm still cracking up. "My *chemistry partner* is a werewolf."

"Shifter—not werewolf."

I use my shoulder to try to wipe the tears of laughter from my face. "What's the difference?"

"Werewolves don't exist. Just in movies. But I don't get it. What's funny?"

"It's like *Twilight*."

Abe sends me a blank look.

"The book? The movie? You know—the new girl's lab partner ends up being a vampire who's attracted to her. My lab partner ended up being a wolf." I blink at him as a new thought occurs to me. "Are you attracted to me? Is that why you've been prowling around my house?"

"I'm not *attracted* to humans," he says gruffly. There's a defensiveness to his tone that makes me certain I'm right.

Abe pulls up in front of a sprawling mansion with iron gates. He rolls his window down to speak to the camera, but the gates swing open before he does.

My sense of misgiving amplifies a hundred times. "Where are we? Is this the drug dealer? Abe, what's happening?"

It's pitch black outside when Abe pulls up in the circle drive and parks the car. His expression is set in a grim line, and his shoulders are tense, like he's bracing against something. He's worried too. Or he has a distaste for whatever he's about to do.

I panic. "Abe, don't do this. I won't tell your secret, I swear. Just take me home. This doesn't feel right."

Abe reaches for a pair of mirrored sunglasses in the center console and, even though it's dark out, puts them on. "It doesn't feel right to me either, to be honest. And yeah, I guess I can tell you now since you won't remember, I'm definitely attracted to you."

He swings his door open and climbs out.

The momentary flicker of triumph at his admission of attraction immediately dies when the other part sinks in. I won't remember this? I won't remember getting to know what's under the school bully's assholery.

How he went out to search for my mom's letter. Or how he held me when I cried. I won't remember that Abe isn't as big of a dick as he pretends to be.

Or that what they say about boys who pick on girls is true—he likes me.

He opens my door.

"I don't like this." My throat is clogged. "What's happening?"

He rips the duct tape off my ankles and picks me up by the waist to lift me out of the SUV and onto my feet. "It's about to get a whole lot more like *Twilight*."

"What do you mean?"

"Werewolves may not exist, but vampires do."

Chapter Seven

A
be
I'm sick to my stomach as I take Lauren's elbow.

She resists me, yanking out of my grasp.

"No. You're not bringing me there. No fucking way."

I'll say one thing about the ice princess—she has good instincts. She's right to balk at this. I'm wrecked over it.

"I'm sorry, Pearls." I swing her up into my arms. She kicks her feet and hits me with her taped hands, but she's no match for me.

"Abe, no! Put me down! Take me home!" She attempts to turn her body and twist out of my arms. The scent of her fear makes my wolf snarl with the need to defend her.

"You're not—" Her words die when the door swings open, and a slender kid in a 1920's blue velvet smoking jacket opens the door.

He looks like he can't be older than Lauren and I, but I'm not deceived. Based on his fashion choices he's probably over 100 years.

"Thomas?" I ask. The scent of the undead makes my skin crawl. I've never seen a leech in person before.

It's scary as fuck.

The vampire barely spares me a glance, but he takes a slow lecherous perusal of Lauren's body, lingering on the soft exposed flesh beneath her breasts. I can't believe I didn't give her a different shirt to wear. What in the fuck is wrong with me?

I lower her feet to the ground, whip my shirt off, and pull it over her head and shoulders. With her wrists bound in front of her, the sleeves hang empty like she's an armless mannequin. I keep my body angled, so the leech can't see the pistol in the waistband of my jeans. The bullets in it are made of silver.

"A wolf pup and a mortal teen on my doorstep. How uninteresting." His gaze snaps to me like a weapon. Of course, it *is* a weapon. "Take off your sunglasses, wolf child."

"*No.*" I say it firmly. I'm wearing mirrored sunglasses. He shouldn't be able to catch my gaze through these and glamour me into doing what he wants.

I don't say *No, sir*, like I would if he were a wolf elder. I'm just here for a transaction. I can't trust this leech. But I don't want to antagonize him—he's dangerous and only out for himself and his kind. The sooner I complete business and get out of here, the better.

My hand itches to reach for my weapon, but I don't. I need to stay cool.

The vampire gives me a chilling smile. "Where is the money?"

I fork over the two thousand bucks I took from my dad's floor safe. That's how much Austin's contact said it would be. I'll have to figure out a way to pay it back before my dad finds out.

Lauren must remember she was trying to escape because she turns to run. I catch her around the waist and spin her back to face Thomas.

The moment he catches her eye, she goes slack in my arms. I don't release her. My heart pounds against her back.

Thomas catches her chin and lifts it. "Did you see a shifter, love?"

Lauren pants, her ribs widening against my chest with each inhale. Her body seems to be immobile, like she's playing freeze tag and becoming a statue.

I try to soothe her by stroking my thumb in a slow circle over the bare skin at her waist. Before we came, I had this fantasy I would ask the vampire to plant happy thoughts in her, to help her feel better about her mom, but now I realize that was idiocy. I don't trust this guy to do anything extra. The second he wipes the wolf memory, we're out of here.

"I see... you were on a cliff. The wolf pup saved you."

Goosebumps stand out on my arms listening to him root through her mind. This is so fucked up. I clear my throat. "Yeah. Tell her it was the human me who saved her, and then we went to the library to study. And then for a drive."

The leech ignores me. "Lover boy has been watching you. Understandable." He leans forward to sniff her neck. Now I'm panting from adrenaline, too. This guy fucking *creeps me out.*

"You have a unique scent for a human. There's something...different about you."

I catch the glint of his elongated fangs, and I yank her backward, out of striking distance.

Fuck! Was he going to bite her? I need to get the hell out of here as soon as this is taken care of.

"Give her to me," he snaps, like he's pissed I just took away his dinner.

I lift my upper lip in a snarl. *My canines get long, too, asshole.* "No." I make the syllable as hard and forbidding as I know how, throwing every ounce of alpha command into it that I can muster.

Once again, he's amused by my defiance. Like I'm some terrible two who just learned to say no.

Before I know what's happening, he grabs my sunglasses from my face at lightning speed, tossing them into the Texas Ranger bush flanking the door.

I inadvertently let go of Lauren to defend myself, and then they're both gone—vanished inside his house with the door slammed shut in my face.

A real wolf-snarl erupts from my throat. The only thing that keeps me from spontaneously shifting into wolf form is the reminder that I have silver bullets.

I draw the gun at the same time I smash the door down with a powerful kick of my foot.

They are nowhere. Damn, that fucker moves fast.

I hear a whimper down the hall, and I barrel down it and bash another door in.

I find Lauren bent backward in Thomas' arms, the fucking leech feeding from her throat.

I step close, so I won't miss and hit Lauren, then aim and pull the trigger. The bullet rips into his shoulder. Thomas howls and drops to the floor, clutching at the bloodless wound.

A silver bullet won't kill a vampire, but it will sap his power and hurt like hell. I aimed for bone, wanting the bullet to remain lodged there long enough for us to get away.

Lauren's already running out the door. I heard a

vampire's saliva drugs their victim, but she seems more than capable of fleeing.

I don't wait to see if Thomas will recover–I turn to follow her down the hall and out the front door. My body seems to celebrate the second I cross the vampire's threshold into fresh air. Lauren's already in the passenger seat, slamming the door shut.

"Do you know what happens when you cross a wolf with a bear?"

Thomas' voice chills me.

I whirl to point the gun at him again as I swiftly walk backward the rest of the way to the driver's seat. He's slouched to one side, propped against the doorframe like he can't hold himself up.

"They say it can kill the mother, and that's true. But that's not why it's forbidden."

I have no fucking idea why this asshole is talking about bears right now. He must be cray-cray. I've heard it can happen to extremely old vampires. This guy didn't seem all that old, but what do I know?

I slide into the seat and dig in my pocket for the keys. "Do you want to know the real reason?" he asks as I reach for the door handle.

I slam it closed but with my shifter hearing, I still hear the vampire's parting words.

"It's forbidden because the resulting animal is too powerful."

I step on the gas and peel out on the brick driveway, smashing through the gate even though it was slowly swinging wide.

It drags along beside the car for a few moments before it falls away and tumbles down the street.

I think we're safe until the cold end of the pistol pokes into my ribs.

"That's it, Abe. I've had it." Lauren managed to pick up the gun in the pocket of her bound hands. "Pull over, or I swear I'll shoot."

Chapter Eight

L*auren*

My junior year at Landhower, Luke got everyone in the Suntan Six ecstasy for a party. The way I feel now is pretty similar. Despite my awareness of what just happened, I'm blissed out, slightly in lust with Abe, and queasy. Which is why I'm doing everything I can to muster anger.

Abe almost got me killed! Or raped. Or permanently kept as a blood slave. I don't know what that vampire's plans were for me, but they couldn't have been good.

But something he did made it so that nothing really bothers me. I felt no trauma or fear when he bit me. Only a pleasant disassociation from everything.

Great. Like I need to feel more numb about my so-called life.

The important thing, though, is that I remember everything. The memory of Abe shifting from wolf to human returned the moment he kicked the bedroom door in. So did the ability to move.

For whatever reason, Abe seems to be the cure to whatever ails me. Maybe it's the turn-on of his dramatic rescue. Or just that he continuously pisses me off. I'm leaning into that righteous anger right now as I point his pistol at him.

My table-turn lasts approximately 2.5 seconds.

Abe apparently isn't afraid of being shot by me because he snatches the gun from my hands and empties the chamber of bullets into his lap as he drives.

"Don't point that thing at me. If that goes off, I could die."

"Yeah, that was kind of the point."

He splits a glance between me and the road. "I'm sorry, Lauren. I really am. That wasn't supposed to happen."

I punch him as best I can with the limited use of my hands. "No shit. Well, I didn't consent to what *was* supposed to happen, so I guess having my vein drained by a vampire was the perfect end to a shitty day."

Abe's gaze lands on the puncture marks at my neck, and he abruptly swerves to the side of the road.

To my shock, he grasps my nape and pulls me toward his mouth.

"What are you doing? Get off me, perv!" I punch his chin as he comes closer. I know I didn't hit him hard, but it's like he doesn't even feel it.

His lips part and press against the skin of my neck. Then he drags his tongue over the place where the vampire bit me.

Oh.

Oh, wow. What is he doing?

My pussy gets wet—*soaking* wet.

I was already turned on by seeing him bash through that door and shoot a gun. It's not every day a kid from high school suddenly transforms into the bad-ass hero from an action movie. But this is next-level.

I've never felt so innervated, so lustful in my entire life.

"Don't flatter yourself, Pearls." Abe's voice is a deep rumble against my skin. "If I were using my tongue for pleasure, you'd be begging me for more." He murmurs the words in my ear, then swirls the tip of his tongue around each of my puncture marks.

The slow pulse between my legs grows more insistent. "Wh-what are you doing, then, creep-o?" I'm too flustered for my epithet to sound even remotely genuine. Too turned on by this big, virile male holding me captive to lick my neck. I become aware of his other hand, which grips my knee. His thumb brushes lightly along the sensitive skin of my inner thigh.

"My saliva has antibiotic and healing properties." Another lick.

I can't stop thinking about his tongue between my legs now. How it would feel if he gave a slow roll of that tongue over my clit the way he's moving it now. *You'd be begging me for more.*

It definitely sounds like Abe Oakley knows what he's doing.

I've only been with one guy–Luke–and I've never begged for more. Yesterday, I would've sworn Abe was the last guy I'd ever get hot for, but right now, I'm wishing I were already single. That I could ask Abe to show me how just exactly he'd use his tongue for pleasure.

"My saliva's not as potent as a vampire's, but it will help heal the wounds."

"O-oh."

Oops. That sounded sexual. More like a moan than acknowledgment. Did I just undulate my hips on the car seat?

I'm not going to admit that I don't want him to stop.

That the pulse between my legs has become louder and louder, and now it's all I can do not to lick him back.

"I guess you're attracted to me, too."

Smug bastard.

I shove him away. "Now who's flattering himself?"

Abe quirks a cocky smile, but the brush of his thumb over my puncture wound is almost tender. "I know the scent of your arousal, Pearls." He touches his nose. "I have an excellent sense of smell."

My cheeks heat. Can that be true? Well, it must be if he said it.

Without ungluing his gaze from mine, he rips off the duct tape on my wrists–the same tape I've been futilely twisting and tugging for the last two hours–with his bare hands. He balls the mess up and shoves it under the seat then pulls his shirt off my head. His gaze falls hungrily on my exposed bra and bare belly.

I try not to be flattered, but my body doesn't get the memo. My nipples stiffen and peak under my bra. Every part of me seems to freaking *love* Abe's attention. And now that he's admitted his interest to me, it's much, much harder to hate him.

It's like the two of us are in on the same secret. I mean, of course we are. Everything that happened tonight is a shared secret. But him saying he's attracted to me was like the turning of a key in a lock.

The activation of an "us". Something we can't return from.

His hand returns to my throat and once more, he strokes his thumb lightly over the place on my neck where the vampire bit me. The second that creature looked into my eyes, I could hear his commands in my head.

Don't move. My body went still.

Then, *You didn't see a wolf tonight.* I tried to think of wolves, but couldn't even picture one.

I "remembered" Abe–in his human form–catching me falling off the cliff, but nothing after.

And then suddenly I was in the vampire's bedroom having my vein drained. But I felt certain Abe would stop him. I didn't believe for a second that he would leave me at the mercy of the blood-sucker.

And I've never seen anything so badass as that door flying off the hinges and a furious Abe coming through. Knowing he was probably scared made it all the more heroic. Knowing he was scared for me was downright swoony.

"Does this still hurt, Lauren?" He's being genuine Abe–not the cocky asshole from school. This is a guy I could actually fall for. Which scares me.

"Of course, it fucking hurts." I shudder, remembering how it felt to be enthralled by the vampire.

I'm lying. It doesn't hurt much at all. I'm still buzzing–feel good hormones rush through my body like I just orgasmed or had a great workout. The heaviness that has surrounded me, the fog I've been living in for the past year, seems to have cleared for the moment.

So there is a gift to this fucked up night.

Also, I cried. That might be the biggest gift of all.

"Take me home, Abe," I say because it's all too much to absorb. Not that Abe is a werewolf or I was bitten by a vampire. No, the part that's really shaking me is my feelings for Abe.

I need to get out of his car. Get home and climb in my bed and just dream this night away. Maybe tomorrow things will make sense.

He puts the car in drive. Neither of us speaks again until he pulls up in front of my house.

I throw the door open to get out, but he grabs my wrist. "Hold up."

I try unsuccessfully to shake him off.

"You say a word to anyone about this–"

"Go fuck yourself, Abe," I tell him.

"No, Pearls." He transforms back into his cocky asshole persona right before my eyes. There's a puffing of his chest. A lift and thrust of his chin. A jeering sort of expression around the mouth.

I want to slap that expression right off his face. I brace for whatever assholery will come from his mouth.

"Here's how it's going to go, princess. I will keep your mom's letter as insurance. If you talk–if you say a word to anyone about what transpired tonight–I will make you watch as I burn it to ashes."

Chapter Nine

A*be*

I prowl closer to the Sterling mansion. It's midnight, but I can't sleep. I popped my window open and crawled out, staying in human form this time as I stalk my prey.

I should be glad I made Lauren Sterling hate me again.

She punched me in the jaw when I threatened her, which didn't hurt me, but probably bruised the hell out of her knuckles.

But it's what needed to happen. Feeling anything resembling closeness to her would be even more of a disaster than her finding out I'm a shifter.

Or getting bitten by a vampire.

No—scratch that—nothing could be worse than that leech touching her. I still want to punch my own throat for putting her in that situation. I regret taking her to that demon. I still want to go back with a fucking stake and drive it straight through his unbeating heart.

But I should leave things the way they are with Lauren.

With her despising me and me having leverage. I shouldn't be back at her window with the letter in my back pocket.

The screen is ripped from where my paw went through on the last full moon. I'm surprised her rich daddy hasn't fixed it yet.

But, then again, he's grieving.

It's harder to scorn these rich humans now that I know they're all suffering. They're not closed off because they think they're too good for the rest of us–they're shut down from grief.

Or maybe it's both.

Probably both. She definitely still has a chip on her shoulder, no matter how you slice the cake.

I catch her scent around the window, and my wolf whines.

I'm not sure what I'm going to do. Leave the letter on her windowsill? Put it in her mailbox? All I know is that my conscience wouldn't rest until I brought the letter here.

I look in the window. My vantage point is different than when I'm in wolf form. On two legs I can see her bed below the window. The sprawl of her thick copper hair across the pillows.

I gently detach the screen and lean it against the house. Then I try the window.

It's unlocked.

Lauren's eyes fly open at the soft sound. I'm about to throw the window wide and hurl myself through to clap a hand over her mouth, but I realize she hasn't moved.

Hasn't parted those full lips to scream.

She's just watching me.

I slide the window open as quietly as possible and boost myself up through it.

Lauren looks gorgeous, her pale legs all tangled up in

the sheets and duvet. She's in a pair of minuscule pajama shorts and a camisole with straps made of the tiniest strings I've ever seen. One swipe of my teeth, and I could slice right through them. Make that fabric fall away from her ripe breasts.

My dick gets rock hard.

She still hasn't moved, even though I'm in her bedroom, stalking her in her own bed.

"What are you doing here?" It's a whisper.

So fucking sweet. Like I have a right to be here. Like I'm not just the bully who has been harassing her since the first day of school.

Only because she doesn't seem scared, because I don't feel unwelcome, I climb up over her on the bed.

Even now, she doesn't scream. Doesn't hit me. Doesn't push me away.

The scent of her arousal nearly makes me groan out loud.

Sweet, sweet human. I want to lick those juices from the source. Part her nether lips with the tip of my tongue and take my time learning how she likes it.

I straddle her hips and frame her head with my fists. "Promise me you won't tell."

Now she's mad—same as she was in my vehicle. It's like she's offended by my lack of trust. Like I should believe in her fidelity to me and my secret.

She bucks her hips underneath me, which has the unfortunate effect of jostling my already swelling junk.

I bite back a groan.

I cage her throat with my hand to hold her down, careful not to squeeze. "Careful, Pearls. You're turning me on."

She goes still, her chest rising and falling. For once, my

defect works in my favor because my wolf eyes can see her perfectly in the dark–even the color rising to her cheeks.

She remains frozen for several breaths like she's waiting to see if I'll do something.

Then she whispers, "I promise."

"Not even Lincoln."

I don't know how close twins are, but it seems like if there was anyone she might tell, it would be him.

"I won't tell him."

I shift, so my grip on her neck becomes a caress, my thumb finding the puncture wounds from the leech.

They're better already than they were a few hours ago, but they still make me want to howl and shift to tear that vampire apart.

I lower my head–slowly, so she can push me away if she wants–to the broken skin and drag my tongue over the wounds once again.

My dick surges against the zipper of my jeans. Having her scent up in my nostrils sends my wolf into a frenzy, desperate to mark her with my scent. It also feels like a hit of a powerful drug. One that makes me feel like I've somehow arrived. Like all the striving to cover up my defect, to maintain my dominant position, is over.

It's no longer necessary.

But that would only be true if I wasn't a wolf.

When I lift my head to look into Lauren's face, she looks drugged, too. "How does it look?" Her husky murmur makes me crazy.

Crazy enough to want to rip the covers out from between us and put my head between her thighs.

"Better." My voice sounds deep and rough to my ears.

"I'll wear a collar tomorrow."

Oh Fate. Now I'm picturing her in a dog collar. Or a

slave collar. The kind made of soft leather with a ring at her throat, so I could attach a leash and pull her around. Order her to her knees to suck my–

Pain pierces my temple, and my vision goes bonkers. I suck in a sharp breath to clear my head. I can't lose control.

Why does this human make my condition so much worse?

I release her throat and reach for my back pocket. "Here." I unfold the letter and lay it on her chest.

"I was a dick. I'm sorry."

She takes the letter between her fingers like it's more precious than a sacred religious text delivered directly from the hand of God.

I get it.

"You *are* a dick."

That's my princess. Always giving it back to me.

But then she says, "Thank you," and everything inside me rearranges. The desire to earn those two words from her a million times more nearly overwhelms me.

I want to kiss her.

Desperately.

To taste that smart mouth and press my tongue between her lips.

I settle for another lick of her neck, even though we both know it's not necessary. But with my face pressed against her skin, with her hair brushing against my ear, I find my home. The place I need to be.

I rock my pelvis into hers, the bulge of my cock fitting into the cradle of her legs. Her shaky breath feathers across my shoulder.

The sound of a door opening down the hall makes me spring up. Someone else in the house is awake. I vault soundlessly through the window.

Lauren sits up in bed, the letter clutched to her chest, her lips parted.

I carefully replace the screen and our eyes lock. My vision comes into perfect focus, and all I see is her. The human is so beautiful, she makes my chest ache.

Her bedroom door opens, and I duck out of sight, waiting with my back pressed to the house until it closes again. Only then do I sprint to the woods with Lauren's scent coating the front of my shirt and my wolf pissed as hell I didn't stay.

Chapter Ten

*L*auren

I must be crazy because I decided to go to the Saturday night football game. Lincoln was going with Rayne, and for some reason, I accepted their invitation to join them.

I told myself it's because I need to get out. Need to make an effort at a social life here. But the truth is that I have this borderline obsessive need to see Abe again.

His visit last night messed with my head. I hated him with every fiber of my being after he told me he was keeping my mom's letter, but then he had to bring it back and apologize. Had to crawl up over me and remind me just how hard and firm his body is...*everywhere.*

After he left, I couldn't stop touching myself, imagining what it would be like to succumb to the temptation of screwing the captain of the football team.

How cliché.

But here I am at his game, needing to know if seeing him will lift the numbness again.

My phone rings, and I look at the screen. Luke. I send it

to voicemail. Now that I've decided I'm going to break up with him when he gets here, I can't stand even pretending anymore. One more week, and he'll be here for Homecoming. I'll deal with him then.

"You smell that?" A girl behind me in the stadium concession line asks.

"Uh-huh," her companion answers. "Smells like money."

I turn, eyes narrowed because I know they're talking about me. Except now I understand their problem with me and my brother a little better. It's not just our money or the fact that we're new that they object to. *It's our species.* We're not one of them.

"Ignore them." Rayne tugs at my elbow.

She must be human, too. That's why she's an outcast at Wolf Ridge High. She's one of the few locals who will talk to us.

Too bad because I would *kill* to talk to someone about what happened yesterday.

Of course, I promised Abe I wouldn't. Besides, even if Rayne were a wolf, I couldn't say anything. Who knows what her obligation to her pack is. She might report me or something. I don't want to be dragged off by another town member to get my mind wiped by a vampire.

I shudder at the memory.

"Are you cold?" Rayne asks.

"No." I take the nachos and sodas I ordered for us all to share, and we walk to the seats Lincoln is saving in the back of the stands. Not that they need saving. Most of the crowd is packed down in front. No one's fighting us for the nose-bleeds. This town is *crazy* about football.

On the sidelines, the cheerleaders build a complex

pyramid that involves bodies being tossed to the top and then flipping down.

It's circus-level, but there's no net beneath them. "What is up with the cheerleaders?" My tone holds a mixture of awe and disgust.

"I know," Rayne says glumly. "Crazy, right?"

"I can't believe they even allow those kinds of tricks at the high school level. I would think it would be a liability risk."

"I don't know. They're all gymnasts. No one ever falls."

Oh. Right! Because they're all superhuman. It's going to take me a minute or two to adjust to this new perspective. I suddenly have so many questions. Like—can they get hurt? How easy is football for Abe? Is it only their team that's comprised of wolf players? Is it our entire team?

Also, I can't believe I just thought *our* with anything related to this school or town.

The football game starts, and I watch the players on the field.

Okay, fine, I watch Abe, our star quarterback. He's beautiful. He has the body of a thoroughbred and the grace and ferocity of a lion. He makes the plays look effortless. Like throwing the ball most of the way down the field with a flick of his wrist takes nothing.

Too bad his teammate, J.J., fumbles when he catches the throw.

Except...did he fumble?

Abe doesn't look that upset about it. Neither do their coaches. People in the stands are cheering like it wasn't a mistake.

A thought occurs to me. Is this game *child's play* for them? Do they have to pretend to screw up because they're playing against human teams?

"So does Wolf Ridge win *every* game they play?" I ask.

Rayne keeps her gaze on the sidelines where her dickwad stepbrother stands barking orders at the team. There's some drama with him being benched from the Duke team, so he's back helping with Wolf Ridge High. Also, there's some drama between him and Rayne. He acts uber-possessive of her, which is weird.

I don't know, maybe they have a thing for each other.

"No," she says, still watching her stepbrother. "The team is good, but they're not undefeated. They do always make it to the State championships, though."

Abe throws another brilliant pass before he gets tackled to the ground. Make that *lets himself get tackled to the ground*. Because he barely moved when the guy first hit, then went down in a graceful swoop.

I recall how it felt to punch him. Like hitting stone—my knuckles are still bruised. But he didn't even blink.

Abe's friend Markley catches the ball and is also tackled smoothly to the ground.

Once again, there's applause in the stands.

"Why is everyone clapping?" I ask.

Rayne darts a look at me. "Oh...um, just the athleticism of it." She shrugs. "You know... just because Abe threw a long pass. This town loves him on the field."

"Right." I grudgingly love him on the field, too. Part of me still wants to hate on him, but it's getting harder to maintain. He truly is a thing of beauty. And now I know he's not as big a dick as he initially comes off as.

"I heard he almost didn't get to play the game because you weren't there to get him through his chemistry lab Friday."

I raise my brows. "What do you mean?"

"You have to maintain a C average to play. Abe thinks

he's above schoolwork, so it's week to week for him. He barely maintains. I think he got benched a few times last year for bad grades."

"Did that upset him?"

"Does anything upset him?" Rayne scoffs.

"It upset the rest of the town, that's for sure. I'm sure his dad had a fit. Abe will never live up to his brother's golden boy image. Part of me thinks that's why he became such a dick over the last few years."

"He didn't used to be a dick?"

Rayne shakes her head. "No. This will sound crazy, but I used to think he was sweet."

Lincoln, who has been ignoring the conversation until now, snorts. "Sweet is not a word I would choose to describe him."

"Me neither," I mutter, but my conscience pricks. Abe has shown some signs of sweet. He went back to the cliff to retrieve my mom's letter. He also shot a vampire for me and returned the letter to me in the middle of the night. Granted, the latter two were to make up for his assholery, so they don't count. But yeah, I can see what Rayne means.

There is some sweet mixed up with all that cockiness.

A gust of wind blows at our backs, providing relief from the heat. Out on the field, Abe looks for an open player to throw the pass. Then, suddenly, his head snaps to the stands.

For some inexplicable reason, my heart starts pounding. I foolishly think he might be looking for me.

Abe doesn't see the player from the other team barreling toward him.

I'm shocked that my instinct is to stand and point, but of course, I don't. I just sit still and watch as he's tackled to the ground.

This time it isn't graceful.

He was definitely play-acting before. The fickle crowd shouts and boos at him.

Abe gets up, then drops back to his knees, clutching the sides of his helmet at his temples.

Now I *do* jump to my feet. "Shut up," I yell at the people booing. "He's hurt!"

* * *

Abe

The pain in my temples blinds me. No, that's backwards–it's my eyes that cause the pain. I could have sworn I caught Lauren's scent in the wind, and my wolf went haywire. I lost focus on the game.

It's the first time I've ever been tackled without letting it happen. I try to climb to my feet but stagger backward and then fall to my knees.

My teammates pay no attention. Hopefully they think I'm faking it. Of course, for appearances, they should also fake concern. Instead, it's a player from the Cave Hills team who puts a hand on my back and leans over. "You okay, man?"

"Yeah," I lie. "I just need a minute."

I still can't see a fucking thing. I suck in deep breaths, trying to get my eyes to focus. And then my dad is suddenly out on the field, holding the sides of my helmet and pulling me to my feet. "I got it. I'm a doctor," he says to the Cave Hills player. To me, he murmurs, "It's okay, son." He leans his forehead against my helmet. "Deep breaths." His voice is so low I almost can't hear it. Of course, my dad's biggest fear is that our family's dirty secret will be found out. That our tainted DNA will come to light, and he'll lose his position on the council.

"I'm trying!" I growl back.

"Okay," he soothes me. "Now, *shift to human form.*" He uses alpha command in his voice to force my body into compliance. I'm already in human form, obviously, but my eyes don't seem to know that.

It works, at least partially. Some of my vision returns at the periphery. Until I catch another sweet note of Lauren's scent, and my wolf goes berserk.

I barely stifle the cry of agony that rockets from my mouth.

"*Human. Form.*" Once more, the alpha command shimmers around my body, sending shivers down my spine, ricocheting out my limbs to my fingers and toes. My joints crack, and my vision resets.

"I'm good." I bob my head to show my dad that I'm back.

"Atta boy. You got this, Abe. Shake it off and kick some ass out there."

"We're not supposed to kick ass today," I mutter.

Coach Jamison and Wilde decided that we should lose this game. Wolf Ridge High can't always be undefeated, or it would draw too much attention to our little town. The coaches let us know right before the game how they want us to play. The outcome remains a secret to the community, so they will still show up to watch the games.

"Well, do it with style, then. And then I want you at my clinic after the game. I need to run tests on you." My dad thumps the side of my helmet and jogs off.

Fuck. More tests. That's my entire relationship with my dad these days.

Still, to make him happy, I turn to the stands and pump my fist in the air. I have to show the school I'm all right. The applause is tepid. Wolf Ridge High and the rest of the community must know that was a real hit because I wasn't paying attention. They want showmanship whether we win or lose. They're here for entertainment, and I let them down.

I will make it up to them later. Right now, I'm scanning the stands.

There. In the back.

I spot Lauren with her twin, Lincoln, along with Rayne the Runt. Except, I'm not supposed to call her that anymore. Wilde has become super protective of his new stepsister. He cornered me in the locker room and told me I have to make sure everyone votes her in as Homecoming Queen.

As if I don't have my own bullshit to spread around and make stick at school. Now I have to figure out how to make his fly, too.

Lauren's looking my way, too. The moment we lock gazes, it's like lightning striking my body. My eye starts to twitch.

Fuck.

I quickly look away. I can't have another episode. Not here. Not in front of everyone, like this.

"Abe, what's up?" Now Wilde is in my face.

I shake my head, trying to shake off the changes Lauren brought over me.

I shrug, even though he won't notice the movement under my shoulder pads. "Just fucking around." I give him my cockiest grin.

He gets in my face. "Well, you look like an asshole. Show a little more grace if you're going to get knocked to your ass, for fucks' sake."

"Come on," I add a massive dose of swagger to my voice. "That was crazy realistic, was it not?"

J. J. snorts.

"It was." Markley fist-bumps me as we jog to our positions on the field.

I do my best to amp up the entertainment for the rest of the game—throwing passes that make my teammates have to do semi-miraculous moves to catch and doing back flips when we make a touchdown.

After the game, students congregate outside the bleachers, making their plans. I'm busy posturing to everyone, making sure no one thinks anything is amiss, but all the while I scan the crowd for Lauren.

No dice.

She and her twin seem to have disappeared.

I see Casey Muchmore presiding over a large group of volleyball players and cheerleaders. She glances over at me. I should go over and ask her to Homecoming.

Full disclosure—we've hooked up a few times during full moon runs. Her older brother Cole would kick my ass to Kansas if he knew, and their dad would probably straight up murder me. The guy used to drink too much and get violent.

The thing is—I don't feel bad because I don't think it means any more to her than it does to me. I think she was curious about sex. So was I.

She was pretty bold about telling me how she wanted it and what she liked. It was fine—I wouldn't say it rocked either of our worlds. I chalk it up to normal teen experimentation. I never for a moment got the impression that she had any emotional attachment to me or expectation that we be anything to each other at school or elsewhere.

So her looking over at me now is almost out of character.

Casey is alpha enough, I'd almost expect her to march over and demand when I'm going to ask her.

Except, she doesn't. For some reason, I get the feeling she hopes I won't.

That doesn't make sense, though. It's expected for us to go together since we would be Homecoming King and Queen.

Would be if I didn't now have to figure out how to make Rayne get voted in as queen without losing face with literally everyone.

River, one of the cheerleaders, turns to look at me, too. Casey immediately touches River's waist in what looks like both a reassuring and possessive touch.

Oh. Don't know why I didn't see that in her before. Maybe she already has a hot date to Homecoming.

"Hey Abe, you driving to the mesa?" J.J. asks.

The popular kids head up there post-game to hang out with the she-wolves around a fire for flirting and fooling around.

"I can't, I'm grounded," I lie. "I'm on probation for grades again." That part is true.

"Bummer. Okay, see you later, man." We fist-bump, and I walk to my Land Rover, scanning the parking lot for a Tesla, even though I know the twins must be long gone.

My dad texts me: ***I'm waiting.***

Okay, fine. I've got to stop this obsession with Lauren Sterling. She's the reason I have to spend post-game in my dad's clinic instead of hanging out with my friends.

She's the reason my condition is getting worse.

If I were smart, I'd bully some other kid in chemistry into switching partners with me and stay as far away from her as I can.

No, if I were really smart, I'd find a different vampire to

wipe her mind and get him to tell her to switch schools or leave town.

A sharp pain jabs at my temples, and I involuntarily groan at the sudden pain.

Fuck. Even thinking of her now brings on an episode. It's getting so much worse.

This girl is going to destroy everything for me—expose my weakness, make me lose my position as alpha, gut my father.

And I don't want it to stop.

I can't seem to put even a minimal distance between us to prevent my complete destruction.

Chapter Eleven

Monday is the Homecoming royalty election. J.J. makes the rounds as class president, passing out the ballots. I already told all the ballers to make sure Rayne wins as queen and instructed them to spread the word.

So far, no one has questioned it.

That's the good thing about having alpha status. When I give an order, it gets blindly obeyed.

That's why maintaining my status is paramount. It keeps anyone from questioning my behavior when I can't read the board or an instruction sheet. When I can't function in the classroom or out on the field.

Even though after last night's tests in my dad's clinic I resolved to avoid Lauren as much as possible, she's like an addiction to me.

I'm looking for her in the hallways as I strut through them with J. J. and Markley. Desperate to catch her scent. To watch those shapely legs strut around in her short shorts and platform heels. To catch every time she tosses that thick copper mane of hers.

Her brother's scent reaches me from around the corner. It doesn't have any effect on me—not the way Lauren's does, but I don't find it an unpleasant scent like I do with the rest of the human population.

He's standing near Rayne. "Like I said, it's just as friends. I'm not looking for a date-date if that's what you're worried about."

"I'd love to," Rayne says.

I stop. "What's this?" I act the part of the asshole, so no one will know I'm desperate for intel on Lauren. "The runt and the new kid are going to the dance?"

J.J. drops a hand on my shoulder. "*Abe.*" He warns, reminding me that Wilde threatened to kick my ass if I harass his new stepsister.

So I turn my attention to Lincoln. "Is it a double-date?"

Lincoln and Rayne stare at me.

Fuck. I was trying not to be too obvious, but now I have to spell it out.

"Who's bringing your sister?"

Lincoln's upper lip curls. Like his sister, he's not afraid of me or the power I wield at this school. "Her *boyfriend.*"

Boyfriend.

Boy. Friend.

Did he just fucking say *boyfriend?*

My wolf goes into a rage, ready to smash a hole in every locker in the hall. "Oh yeah?" I fight to keep control of my voice. My vision is already going haywire, pain locking into both temples and running down the back of my neck into my shoulders. "*Who is that?*"

I'm going to find the asshole who asked Lauren to the dance and rip off both of his ears. I'm going to—

"None of your business, Abe." Rayne slams her locker and grabs Lincoln's arm to tug him away with her.

"Watch it, Ru...Rayne." I can't see either of them. The entire hallway has turned a smoky black, and I can only see in the edges of my periphery.

I have kids at this school trained to part when I come through, and it works in my favor now because a little squeak from someone leaping out of the way tells me I almost hit a wall.

I use my hearing and sense of smell to navigate my way to my next class. I accidentally sit in the chair next to my assigned place, but the guy who belongs there says, "Yeah, have my chair, bruh."

I paste a cocky grin on my face as I jump up. "Just kidding, man." I move to the correct seat.

I will myself not to think about Lauren.

About the fucking *boyfriend* who is taking her to Homecoming.

About what my wolf wants to do to the guy.

I need to make it through this week, so I can play the game on Thursday night, or my dad will never forgive me. That means I can't look at, talk to, or even breathe around the ice princess.

If I do, there's no telling what my wolf will do.

* * *

Lauren

The slight fizz of interest I had in seeing Abe at school quickly goes flat Monday afternoon. He wears a surly, dickish expression in Chemistry and, for the first time, ignores me.

I'm used to his bullying. The attention he throws my

way–even though it was jabs and sneers. I'm unaccustomed to him pretending I don't exist.

I'm not hurt. I'm way too disaffected to feel anything resembling caring about the situation. But the little spark of life Abe brought to my system this weekend dies out. I'm back to full numbness.

Back to wondering if it will ever clear or lift. If I'll ever be human again.

And I have Homecoming and breaking up with Luke to contend with this coming weekend.

Yay.

Abe's jerkiness continues all week. I try to reconcile this new version of him, not with the old school persona but with the guy whose chest I cried on. The guy who admitted he's attracted to me. The guy who climbed through my window and pinned me down in my bed. Got me wet just from the feel of his hard muscles and imagining what it would be like to have him inside me.

Now, I almost wonder if I imagined the whole damn thing.

Maybe I'm going nuts. I needed to feel something so badly I invented a werewolf and a vampire and a hot kidnapping by the jock at school. I look for evidence of werewolves in every class, but I see nothing to confirm or deny my experience.

On Thursday, we're in the lab together with a new assignment. Abe stands at a distance from me, his body tense and rigid, his nostrils flaring. I try to erase the memory of how those glorious muscles look beneath the casual t-shirt and khakis.

"Are you going to pull your weight today?" I snark.

He just shrugs.

Damn him.

I actually miss our usual banter–the two of us poking at each other and posturing, but Abe still looks murderous. Like I'm the one who did him wrong instead of the other way around.

Here I was going to forgive him for kidnapping me and letting a vampire suck my blood. Trying to wipe my memories of him.

If any of that even happened...

Now I'm pissed as hell.

I'm not about to do this lab by myself and let him get the credit again. I heard what Rayne said—he almost didn't get to play in the last game because I wasn't in class to help him with the lab. Well, tonight is the Homecoming game, so if he wants to play, he'll have to pass this lab.

I put on my protective goggles. Normally, I'm the one who mostly ignores him while he tries to get a rise out of me. Now I go on the offensive. "Let's go, hotshot." I push the instruction sheet across the lab table toward him.

A muscle tics in his cheek, but then he lifts his chin to look down his nose at me. The swagger returns. Now I know for certain it's something he puts on and off. Something he wears like his Varsity letterman jacket.

"I'm not your pool boy, Pearls."

There he goes, making it about my money again. Turning it back around on me when he's been the one treating *me* like the errand girl.

I shrug my shoulders and give him a *whatcha-gonna-do?* smile. "I'm not going to do your work for you anymore, quarterback. So if you want to play in tonight's game, I guess you better figure out how to get this lab done."

I note the unease on his face before he hides it. I was right. He needs me way more than he's been letting on.

"Really?" His voice drips with exaggerated doubt. "You're going to take an F on today's lab, Ms. Straight As?
"

"I can fake period cramps, leave, and make it up later like I did with Friday's lab. But you don't have that luxury, do you?"

He pushes his tongue in his cheek, his eyes narrowing.

I spread my hands. "So go ahead, big shot. Show me how it's done." I pick up the instruction sheet and wave it in his face.

He snatches my wrist, pulling me against his body. His other hand ghosts over my hip, lighting up every nerve ending in its vicinity. We're close enough I feel the heat of his body through my clothes.

"Careful, Pearls," he murmur-growls. "You never know what might happen if you get this close to me." His eyes glow ice blue. His wolf is showing. How many times did I miss seeing the truth before?

At least I know for sure that I'm not going crazy.

"We wouldn't want something to happen that would upset your *boyfriend* back home, now would we?" He spits the word *boyfriend* like it poisoned his tongue.

My mouth drops open with surprise.

Well—what do you know? Abe's jealous. Now his anger makes sense.

Someone must've told him I have a date to homecoming. Lincoln or Rayne, since I don't talk to anyone else at this school.

It explains why he's been so pissy with me all week.

If he hadn't been such a dick, I might let him off the hook and tell him the truth about Luke's visit. But I don't owe him that. I don't owe him anything.

So I just reach up, pull his goggles away from his forehead and release them, so they snap down on his nose. "That's right, we wouldn't."

His eyes flash ice blue again. His grip tightens on my hip, fingers twisting up the fabric of my jean shorts.

With a roar, my body comes back to life. The black and white lab turns to color. Sensation kick-starts. My nipples tingle, a slow, hot thrum sounds between my legs.

My breath stalls.

He's not breathing either.

It's like the two of us are suspended in time, our angry gazes locked on one another. He's still holding my wrist, and his thumb begins to move over my pulse there. He slowly draws my hand toward his mouth. His lips part.

They are sensual lips for a guy–full and supple. I wonder what it would be like to be kissed by him.

He bites my knuckle. Not hard but not soft.

A weird, warbling sound comes from my mouth. Something like, *Ahh...oh.*

I have no idea what he means by the bite. Was it punishment? Seduction? A warning?

All I know is that it feels like lightning struck my spine. Tingles ignite everywhere. I'm flushed with heat, hungry for more.

He's finally managed to do what he's been attempting since the first day of school–discombobulate me.

I yank my hand out of his grasp and search his face.

A slow, cocky grin appears.

Damn him.

I should walk out. Leave him to figure out this lab on his own. But something won't let me move.

Abe releases my wrist and my waist in slow increments, so I barely notice when I'm free.

He pushes the instruction sheet across the counter

toward me. For some reason, he thinks he's won. Because he got under my skin. Mastered me.

Since my feet are refusing to walk away, I turn my attention to the lab—where it should've been this whole time, anyway. I pull down the beakers and test tubes.

"How much of the solution do we need?" I ask.

Abe glances down at the paper, squints, and looks back up. Then he takes the solution from me—not in a gentlemanly way, more of a snatchy, *mine* kind of way. "You tell me," he challenges.

I stare at him, trying to figure out this confusing-as-hell guy. And that's when I realize what I should've figured out weeks ago when he began this whole game of making me do all the work for him.

Abe might actually *struggle* with schoolwork. What if it's not just laziness? He could be like the college athletes you hear about who never learned to read above a third-grade level and somehow fake it through or get passed through because of their physical prowess. Or maybe he can't read at all.

I remember him squinting at the text on my phone the same way.

Could he be dyslexic? Or neurodiverse in some other, undiagnosed way?

Or maybe it is diagnosed, but he doesn't want anyone to know. He could be the classic bully—using fronting and intimidation to cover up his own perceived weakness.

Huh.

It's an interesting thought. If I'm right, it would make him less detestable.

I drop the condescension and just pretend he's a normal lab partner who is willing to share the work. I give him instructions and narrate out loud what I'm doing.

And...he follows along.

In fact, he seems somewhat relieved.

Well.

I learned something new.

We finish the lab with perfect results, and Ms. Miller walks over to praise us.

When she walks away, Abe takes off his goggles and folds his arms over his chest in his patently cocky way. "You're good at this, Pearls."

You're not. I don't say it out loud.

I have a lot more compassion for him suddenly. Even though he's a royal ass most of the time, at least I understand him more now.

"I guess you get to play ball tonight after all." The bell rings, and I pick up my backpack.

"I'll see you there." He gives me a Hollywood-worthy smirk followed by a wink.

I'm fascinated by my own flutter of interest in response. These signs of life he brings out in me. "I'm not going," I say to his departing back.

He turns, his smile growing. "Oh, you'll be there."

Chapter Twelve

A*be*

"*Shift.*"

I'm naked on the floor of my dad's clinic with electrodes taped to my head.

Again.

The moon is nearly full, and I had another episode during the Homecoming game after I was crowned king with Rayne the Runt as queen.

I shift into wolf form at my father's command. He's not looking at me, he's watching the readouts on his screen.

"Now shift back."

Naked again. I don't bother to stand up.

"What were you thinking about when you had the episode?"

I try not to think about Lauren's candy-apple scent. Or what seeing her in the back of the stands did to me.

A blinding pain hits my right temple, and I groan.

"There. That was it. What are you thinking about now?"

"Nothing," I grunt. "Just the game."

Rayne didn't even come down to get her crown. It could've been fucking Lauren as my queen.

That might have settled my wolf a little. Knowing I could take her from the boyfriend I need to kill and have her in my arms for a dance. My wolf has been out of his mind all week. My episodes are getting more frequent. I can barely see at school now, just knowing she's in the building.

I've had to run in the woods every night, scratching at trees and boulders to release my pent-up aggression. Prowling the perimeter of the Sterling mansion. No one has been there. I haven't caught any new scents.

Maybe Lincoln just said there was a boyfriend to fuck with me?

But that would mean he knows I care about Lauren, which would be another huge problem.

I barely restrained myself from violence against the other team tonight thinking it could be one of them. Unlikely, but you never know.

It's not anyone from Wolf Ridge, or I would know it.

The only thing that's given me relief was getting my hands on her today in Chemistry. That moaning, needy sound that came from her lips when I bit her knuckles.

Her scent told me that no matter who this clown is she calls a boyfriend, I'm the guy who turns her on. The one she's thinking about when she touches herself at night.

If she touches herself at night.

Oh, fates... I roll my hips toward the floor to hide my sudden boner.

"That's it! You did it again." My dad is fortunately still looking at his screen. "What are you thinking about right now?" He's excited, like he's on the brink of solving my genetic defect.

"Nothing," I pant. The pain hits behind both eyes and

at the base of my skull. My stomach squeezes tighter than a fist.

My dad turns from the screen, his rolling chair creaking with the movement. "You're lying."

There's danger in his tone. My dad is laid back compared to other male shifters. He wields a quiet authority without needing to back it with physical aggression. I always chalked it up to his attending college and med school with humans. And of course, his family practice only treats humans, since shifters rarely get sick or hurt. He's had to blend in with humans and show a gentler side.

But this defect of mine is the one thing that sends him over the edge. And he smelled the lie.

I squeeze my eyes shut, trying to push away the pain. I'm not about to tell him about Lauren. I've already been warned to stay away from her by our alpha.

And my dad doesn't want me to even *think* about a human female.

The moment we figured out I had the family defect, he started drilling into my head the need to mate with an alpha she-wolf.

Forget about finding your fated mate. You lock down the most alpha female you can find as soon as possible and start breeding her. We need to clear our line of this defect, he always told both me and Austin.

Of course, I argued it made more sense for me not to have pups at all, but he disagreed. He wants to conquer this thing by breeding it out of our line.

It's weird and fucked up but, basically, his entire purpose in life. His mother had it, and it's the reason he became a doctor.

"It's just the full moon," I grunt.

My dad is silent. He knows I'm still lying. I expect him

to get up and stand on me. Use alpha command to make me talk.

Seconds tick by. I master my breathing. My vision starts to clear. I open my eyes.

My dad's head is cradled in his hands in a vision of defeat.

His disappointment is so much fucking worse than his anger.

"I'll get it under control," I promise without any hope of it being true.

"You have to, son."

"I will."

"I'm trying to help you, but if you want me to back off, I will."

My eyes burn. "No." I sound strangled. "I appreciate it, Dad. I just... I think I need to run right now."

"Run *where*?" His voice is sharp, like he knows what I'm planning.

Suspects where I've been going every night when I sneak out my window. Knows that I need to get close enough to Lauren to catch her scent again.

I drag myself to my feet. I can only see out of my periphery, but I'm getting better and better at hiding it. "Just out." I bounce on the balls of my feet. "I need to release my aggression from the game."

"Go on, then." He sounds tired. Like he regrets ever having me and passing this gene deficiency on.

I pull on my clothes.

Fuck. If my dad is this disappointed in me for something I can't control, how would he feel if he found out I've been defying him? That my wolf covets a human?

A human who has seen my wolf.

Worse still, I failed to wipe her memories and have no

leverage over this girl. It's not like she loves me or even cares. She has a *boyfriend,* for fuck's sake. Some guy I might *actually* kill if I can't get my wolf under control.

* * *

Lauren

Luke rolls down the window, letting hot air into the Tesla Lincoln and I share. "Let's stop at my cousin's frat house on the way. He said they were having a low-key party tonight."

I'm having the worst fishbowl experience I've had since my mom died.

Lincoln and I picked up Luke from Sky Harbor Airport after the Homecoming game, and it's now close to midnight. I brought Lincoln and made him drive because I wasn't ready to see Luke alone or even to sit in the front seat with him. The whole thing is so freaking awkward. I've put off breaking up for so long that no matter when I do it now, it's going to feel like the wrong time.

It's fine because the two of them are good friends. Or they were when we lived in Manhattan.

"Nah, man. It's a school night for us." Lincoln saves me from answering. "Also, Tempe is in the opposite direction from Wolf Ridge."

"How far?" he demands, pulling a vape out of his pocket and sucking on it.

Lincoln steps on the accelerator and our electric car leaps forward, instantly cutting the distance between us and the car in front of us on the highway. "I don't know—at least forty-five minutes, maybe an hour. You could Google Map it."

"You guys should take off school tomorrow. What am I supposed to do all day?" Luke complains.

"I told you when you booked the flight not to come until Friday," I remind him from the back seat. "You said you could entertain yourself. Looks like you get to hang out with our dad."

"That's cool, Joe loves me. He can show me the Arizona sights."

I barely restrain myself from rolling my eyes. But Luke is right. Our dad does love him since he's the son of his Wall Street attorney and golf buddy.

"Or I could get an Uber to ASU to see Eric." Luke is texting with his cousin, a student at ASU with a double major in partying. I think half the reason he insisted on flying out here for my Homecoming was for the opportunity to hit the college parties with his cousin. I'm not sure what he thinks he'll find there. What would be so much better than the parties he already goes to back East?

"He says they're having a huge party Saturday night. We could blow off Homecoming and go there."

Lincoln gives a non-committal grunt.

I should jump at the opportunity not to go to a Wolf Ridge High event. It's not like I care about dressing up and being seen by anyone there.

The twist in my solar plexus says otherwise, though.

I remember Abe's jealousy about my Homecoming date. The thought fills me with a spreading heat, like when you take a shot of whiskey and choke on the fire.

And even though I owe him nothing, I *do* feel guilty about being with Luke right now. Like I'm cheating on Abe, a guy I've never even kissed. A guy who acts like he hates me at school because of my very species.

What a dick.

Except now I can't stop thinking about Abe. He occupies my thoughts the entire ride home while Luke drones on about our old friends back home, filling Lincoln in on the gossip he's already shared at least three times with me. The longer he talks, the more disconnected I feel from my old life. The names are familiar. Luke's voice and stories are familiar, but I was a different person when I was a part of that life. I may hate everything about Arizona, but nothing about my old life resonates anymore.

We wind our way up through Wolf Ridge to the top of Moongaze Hill. I can't help but scan the darkness that surrounds our driveway for a flash of fur.

The hairs on the back of my neck prickle, but I don't see anything. Still, I feel certain Abe is out there watching. I've seen him every night this week.

It's what took the bite out of Abe being such a prick at school. I love knowing he's this obsessed with me that he prowls around my house every night after bedtime.

Lincoln parks in the three-car garage that sits underneath the house, and the three of us head up the stairs.

"Hey, Joe. Long time, no see." Luke adopts a dopey jocular tone as he shakes my dad's hand.

I cringe at what he must see. My dad, once a powerful hedge fund manager now looks like an old, underemployed man. He's unshaven, greeting a house guest in his pajamas and a bathrobe—something he never would have done before Mom died. His once proud shoulders are now stooped and rounded, and his hair has turned salt and pepper. There's an air of defeat and depression that surrounds him.

Luke knows our dad attempted suicide after our mom died, and the move to Arizona was our attempt to keep him alive. I shouldn't be embarrassed.

It's just that I can already hear him relaying the news back to everyone at Landhower. How sad it is that our dad is barely functional now. How pathetic our lives are in hot, dusty Wolf Ridge.

To escape the scene, I walk to one of the giant picture windows that surround the main floor of the house and look out toward the tree line. I'm numb again like I'm trapped inside of a snow globe and can't get out.

Abe is the only one who ever cracks it open for me.

There.

I catch the reflection of a pair of ice-blue eyes. My heart rate speeds up. The snow globe breaks, and the plasma oozes out. I'm awake again.

Alive.

The corners of my mouth turn up.

"What is it, Lauren?" My dad's voice is sharp. "Do you see that wolf again?" He's obsessed about the wolf situation, which is a problem now that I know it's Abe.

"What wolf?" Luke asks. "The one that tried to come through your window?"

Dammit. Now I wish I'd never told anyone about that. Wish I hadn't screamed and woken up the whole house when it happened.

Lincoln comes to stand beside me at the window.

"No, there's nothing here." I reach for the remote that controls all the drapes in the living room.

"Yes, there is–I saw something move!" Lincoln says. "Is it a grey?"

Fuck.

"Get the rifle there behind the door!" my dad instructs, and Luke lunges for it. "The Fish and Game Department hasn't done a damn thing about putting that rabid beast down. I'm going to kill it myself."

Apparently, Luke wants to be the hero, though. He throws the door open, rifle in hand. I don't know if he even knows how to shoot the thing.

"No, wait!" I try to scoot out the door first, but the two of us get caught in the doorframe together, the long rifle between us.

A snarl sounds from the shadows.

"Wait!" I cry again, running down the steps and out to the landscaped path.

"Stay back, Lauren." Luke is living out some kind of hero fantasy right now.

Over my shoulder, I see him running behind me, pointing the rifle wildly in my direction.

This time, the snarl sounds right in my ears. No—over my head. Because the wolf—Abe—soars through the air and tackles Luke to the ground with two massive paws on his shoulders.

The rifle clatters out of his hand and goes off.

I scream, looking around wildly to make sure no one was hit.

My dad runs for the rifle.

My scream draws Abe's head around, and he and I both freeze, our gazes locked. "*Go,*" I mouth.

My dad picks up the rifle and aims.

"*No!*" I shout.

And then Abe moves, faster than I would've dreamed possible, bounding back into the cover of darkness and boulders and scrub.

I let out a slow sob of relief.

As my breath slows, I relish the sensation of my heart thudding against my breastbone. Knowing that I *do* care about something in this world.

If not my life, his.

Not the guy I should be worried about. The guy I've called boyfriend for the last year and a half. The one crawling to his feet and dusting off his designer jeans.

No, I'm not worried about Luke for a moment.

All my fear is for Abe.

He's still the only one who reminds me I'm alive.

I may be barely functioning, a mere glimmer of my old self, but Luke's visit shows me it's not my old self I seek. There's someone new emerging from this husk of a life. Someone only Abe can spark to life.

Someone only Abe can nurture.

Like it or not, my destiny is somehow intertwined with his.

Because for the first time since I moved to this hot, desolate town, I realize I want more.

More of the silver wolf with ice-blue eyes who stalks me at night.

More of the guy who crawled through my window to return my mom's letter.

More of whatever he wants to do with me.

Chapter Thirteen

Abe

Fuck!

Fuck, fuck, fuck!

I race through the brush on four paws, the acrid stench of that human's fear still up in my nose.

I completely blew it. I attacked a human! Even worse, a human *at the Sterling Mansion.* The place I was forbidden by my alpha to return to.

I never meant to reveal myself, but when I saw that idiot point the rifle at Lauren, my wolf lost it. The human is lucky I didn't tear his throat out. It was only Lauren's scream that brought me back and kept me sane. I turned to make sure she was safe, and our gazes locked.

For my wolf, that recognition hits bone deep. She saw me. Knows me as a wolf. Was afraid...*for me?*

It's ironic that she would be the one to calm me when she causes my wolf to lose his shit on a daily basis.

Despite the world of trouble I'm going to be in with my dad and Alpha Green, I'm not sorry I knocked that shithead on his ass. He must be the fucking boyfriend.

He smells like expensive cologne and East Coast assholery. He must be the fuckface who thinks he's good enough to take Lauren to Homecoming. I still would like to pry his eyeballs out and shove them down his throat.

I race to the back of my house and in through the dog door. Like all the properties of the pack royalty, our house abuts pack land, so we can shift and run straight from home.

The lights are on, and I hear my parents up, talking in the kitchen. Could the word of my attack have already reached them? My stomach knots like a fist under my rib cage.

I shift to human form and yank on a pair of sweatpants.

"Abe?" My mom calls out.

"Hi, Mom." I walk into the kitchen, forcing a relaxed posture into my jerky limbs.

"Son." My dad's voice is somber.

My mom says, "Abe, little Rayne Lansing went missing during the game tonight. Have you seen or heard anything about her?"

"Wh-what?" I'm so braced for trouble of my own making, this comes as a surprise.

"Remember how she didn't come to take her crown at half-time?" My mom reminds. "She ran out of the stadium when it was announced, and no one has seen her since."

"Oh, wow." I'm still barely processing what she's saying. Still recovering from nearly killing a guy ten minutes ago. I move to the refrigerator and pull out chicken leftovers. Dinner was so long ago, I could eat five chickens right now.

"Speaking of which... how did it happen that Rayne was voted in as queen?" My mom gives me a sharp look. "I heard you might have had something to do with it. Were you trying to hurt her?"

I pick up the chicken with my fingers, eating it cold. "What? No." Now I'm getting in trouble for something I didn't do. Which, frankly, is a relief. "Mom, Wilde told me to make it happen for her, so I made it happen. I guess he's taking his role as her new big brother seriously."

"I'm not sure that's how it is," my dad mutters.

"What do you mean?" My mom turns wide eyes on him.

"I mean, Wilde nearly tore the Sheriff's office apart when he reported her missing."

I cock my head, not understanding.

My mom gasps. "You mean–"

My dad nods. "Mates. I'd put my money on it."

Goosebumps rise on my arms although I'm not sure why. Witnessing Fate at work, maybe. Fate matching an alpha like Wilde with the runt of the pack–a girl who's more defective than I am. She can't even shift.

Fate threw step siblings together as mates. It's crazy and wrong and yet also sort of perfect. I mean, there they are, under the same roof with each other. It would be impossible to resist their animal nature. Would Wilde ever have come near a little runt like Rayne otherwise? Hell, he's supposed to be away at college right now, but he was suspended from playing. Fate orchestrated his return to Wolf Ridge to stay at the house where Rayne now lives.

"Son." My dad's tone is serious. "We think Rayne was kidnapped."

My brows shoot up. "Kidnapped? Why?"

"Her scent disappeared on the sidewalk leaving the stadium. Like someone picked her up."

"Whoa."

"Sit down. I'll heat that up for you," my mom says.

"No, this is fine." I wave her back to her chair.

"There's more," my dad says. "Word has been spreading about this underground group called the Venators."

More goosebumps crawl over my arms although this time, it's an icy chill of foreboding. Like my wolf knows the danger I'm about to hear.

"They're a secret society of powerful humans who know our secret. They hunt shifters."

I stop chewing, a dark rage brewing in my belly. "That's fu–messed up."

"They go after adolescents who haven't shifted yet. They keep the young as prisoners until they hit puberty and shift. Then they hunt them before they can control themselves or know their own animals."

My mom's eyes well with tears. "It's awful. I want to hunt every one of them."

"So do I," my dad growls.

"But why do you think they took Rayne? Do they know she can't shift?"

"Maybe. But there is often someone on the inside selling these kids out. So it's possible they know and hope she's just a late bloomer."

A low growl rumbles in my chest. "That's sick." I can't imagine anyone betraying his own kind. I shake my head. "No Wolf Ridge wolf would sell out Rayne Lansing. No way."

"Maybe not a wolf," my mom says ominously.

"Someone scented a bear shifter in our territory this week." My dad looks grim.

The bear. The bear who had Lauren's letter.

Oh, Fate. I swallow.

I didn't tell anyone about seeing him because then I

would have to explain the situation–something I couldn't do. But what if I had said something, and it prevented Rayne from being taken?

Guilt gathers in a pit of my stomach like oil in a pothole.

If something happens to her, I will never forgive myself. She may be the runt, but she's still pack.

"Yeah, I caught that scent, too. I'm sorry I didn't say anything. I should have." I bare my throat in a sign of submission to show my remorse.

"It's okay, son. You couldn't have known something like this would happen. But, yes, you should let a pack elder know anytime you scent something that doesn't belong on our land."

"Yes, sir."

"You didn't smell it tonight?" My mom asks.

I shake my head. "Not a fresh scent."

My dad nods. "Tomorrow, we will all go out and comb the woods. You can skip school. If we don't find that girl soon, she may be dead."

"You think the bear took her?" It doesn't feel right to me.

That shifter had a perfect opportunity to snatch me if he wanted, and he didn't. In fact, he handed over Lauren's letter after I appealed to him. But maybe I don't fit the profile of the kind of young shifter the Venators want. I'm too many years past my awakening.

But I can't exactly tell my parents about any of that now, can I? Not without the rest of the story coming out. And there's no way in hell I'm telling anyone that Lauren knows. There's no way in hell I'll let anyone bring her to another vampire. She doesn't deserve that shit. I will never forgive myself for putting her through that in the first place.

My dad frowns. "He may have taken her, or he may be an informant to the Venators. Either way, I want to track that fucker down, and when I do, he's a dead bear."

"Yeah," I agree, the weight of all my recent fuck ups bearing down on my shoulders like two tons of wet cement.

Chapter Fourteen

Lauren

"This is so ghetto." Luke looks around the Homecoming dance with distaste.

Wolf Ridge High's Homecoming is not held at a fancy hotel ballroom like Landhower's, but at–wait for it–the *town brewery,* where everyone's parents work.

Yep. You heard that right. Another sign of the weird incestuousness of this town. Which, I guess, makes sense if they're all werewolves. No *if.* They *are.*

I look around at the crowd, trying to find evidence of their animal nature. I suppose from the outside it looks like any high school dance–except far less formal than the ones I'm used to back East. Some people are all dressed up, some students are in flip-flops.

I'm in a form-fitting teal dress that matches my eyes and a pair of fuck-me pumps, not that anyone will be fucking me tonight. I still haven't broken it off with Luke, but I have managed to avoid us getting intimate. He must know it's coming.

"At least it's not in the school gym," I mutter. While I

completely share Luke's low opinion of the event, a thread of defensiveness tightens above my belly button.

"You would hope there'd be beer to drink if we're at their brewery." Luke scans the exits and entryways. "Do you think we could get into the factory from here?"

"We already have alcohol," I say in a bored tone. "Speaking of which, I need a swig." I'm beyond numb after a weekend of enduring Luke and every reminder he brought of who I used to be.

Lincoln ditched school Friday and, thankfully, entertained Luke. I seriously owe him. Big time. They went to a party at ASU last night, and we all went shopping in Scottsdale today, so I've been able to avoid intimacy with Luke until now. But it's time.

Not for intimacy. For the break-up talk.

I doubt the alcohol will help, but I need something to break me out of this deadened state. I hold my hand out for Luke's engraved silver flask which he filled with my dad's Grey Goose before we left for the dance.

He pulls it out of his Armani suit jacket pocket and hands it to me. His other hand settles lightly on my hip.

I shimmy out of his grasp, angling my body toward the wall to hide the rather obvious alcohol drinking from teachers and chaperones. The alcohol burns as it shoots down my throat, making my eyes water.

There. I felt that. Except it's more like I'm *observing* myself feeling it, rather than actually experiencing the sensation in my body. Does that mean I'm out of my body? Disassociated with it?

I probably need a therapist. Lincoln and I have been trying so hard to get our dad to talk to someone. Maybe I should lead by example.

My brain instantly goes to Abe. *He* makes me feel. I

savored the hit of adrenaline I got after Abe tackled Luke to the ground outside my door Thursday night. The revving up of my cells. The spark to my libido.

Of course, it was all kinds of wrong, but something in me found it delicious.

I don't mean to, but I find myself searching the room for him again. I saw him when we came in—saw the murderous glances he sent our way.

I'd be lying if I said I didn't enjoy them.

I'd also be lying if I complained about the way his broad shoulders fill a suit jacket. Or how his muscular ass looks as he struts around in those pants. It's sinful. And he came to the dance alone. That was the first thing I noted when we arrived. At least, I haven't seen a girl on his arm.

"I seriously hope they didn't pay for this D.J.," Luke complains. "My twelve-year-old brother could have put together a better playlist."

"It's abysmal." Lincoln takes the flask from my hand and takes a deep drink. "How long do you guys want to stay?"

He and Rayne were going to come to Homecoming as friends, but it turns out she and her stepbrother are an item and came out to their parents. Also—in more crazy drama this weekend—we found out she went missing after Thursday night's game, but her stepbrother found her. I'm not sure what the deal is.

I'm guessing I was wrong, and Rayne *is* a wolf, too, because everybody's tight-lipped about it. Half the student population, including Abe, were missing from school Friday—maybe looking for her.

A group of girls come over and surround Lincoln. I guess his human-ness isn't quite as offensive as mine.

"So this is who you endure being around every day."

Luke looks down his nose at the girls talking to Lincoln. They're no less beautiful than girls from Landhower, they just aren't wearing Gucci and Prada and trying to outdo one another with money.

A few weeks ago, I would have joined him in the Wolf Ridge bashing. Now, I'm feeling oddly protective of everyone here.

There's an announcement about the Homecoming royalty coming out to the floor. Luke automatically starts to lead me out there, and I have to tug his arm to stop him. "It's not us."

The look of disgust on his face grows louder.

Rayne and her stepbrother take the floor, creating a wild buzz of scandalized murmurs. My eyes are on Abe, though.

He has some cheerleader's hand in his, and the way she stares up at him with total adoration makes me want to puke. He's not looking at her, though. He's looking at–

Our gazes lock. Gaze is the wrong word, though. More like glare.

The fog starts to lift from me. Heat starts in my core, building there. Tingles race up my arms.

"Let's get out of here." Luke loops an arm around my back and leads me toward the door.

I have to resist the instinct to look over my shoulder at Abe. I already know he's watching.

No part of me wants to leave the dance. It's pathetic and awful and full of strangers and people I hate, but leaving with Luke would signify a choice.

Rejecting this town and my new life in favor of the old one.

The one that doesn't exist or work anymore.

"Luke–" We're at the door. I slow down, making him turn.

Impatience flickers on his face. "Lauren, seriously. Why are we even here?"

I step back, out of his grasp. We're blocking the doorway, but I ignore the people trying to get through. "I didn't want to come to this dance—you did, Luke."

"Well, I didn't know it was going to be so *lame*." He searches my face with exasperation. "What's happened to you?"

Guilt sits like a weight on my chest. My shoulders sag. I can't put it off any longer. I walk through the doorway.

Luke follows. "What's going on with you, babe?"

The *babe* grates on me like biting into tin foil. I keep walking until we get to the Tesla, then I stop and turn. This shouldn't be so hard.

We're not even close anymore.

It's just that Luke was there for me when my mom died. Granted, he sort of fed on the drama of the thing. I think I was more the society princess to him rather than a real person. With some time and distance, I now see that my pain was currency he used to prop up his own importance. He did a lot of bragging to the other kids that he was at the hospital with us when she passed, and that he was one of the pallbearers at the funeral.

"You wanted us to break up in person," I say. "I guess this is it."

"I didn't want us to break up at all." He shoves a hand through his highlighted blond hair. "I don't understand what's happened to you."

"I'm sorry, Luke. I'm just in a weird—"

"I don't even know who you are right now," he interrupts. "You're wearing the same dress you wore to last year's Homecoming. You took me to a dance at a fucking *brewery*.

You didn't even get your hair and makeup done professionally. What has happened to you?"

I blink. Those are his takeaways? Not that we've grown apart. Not that I seem lifeless and flat. Not that I've been a terrible girlfriend–which I have–but that I didn't buy a new dress and go to a salon to prepare for the dance?

"Sorry I didn't go all out for our *break-up date*," I spit with sarcasm and start marching away.

"Where in the hell are you going?" He catches my arm, yanking me back.

I stumble in my Jimmy Choo heels, falling into Luke with my hands out, ready to push him away.

As it turns out, it's not necessary.

A strong arm loops around my waist, and I'm lifted from the ground. "Let go of her."

* * *

Abe

It takes everything I have in me not to shift and sink my teeth into this asshole's flesh.

Instead of releasing Lauren, the guy tightens his grip. "Ow." She tries to yank her arm away.

The sound of her distress sends my wolf into a frenzy. I don't quite manage to stop the unearthly growl in my throat. When I speak, my voice is deadly. "Don't make me kill you, bro."

Lauren's now ex-boyfriend must hear the murder in my voice because he lets go.

I pivot her body away, putting my bulk between her and the threat.

"Whoa, okay," Lincoln calls out, jogging toward us. "Looks like it's time to leave the party."

"Who the fuck is this?" The guy demands, looking down his nose as he gives me an up and down sweep. Rich boy looks like he spends his days calling to the butler to pat his ass.

I'm her fucking mate. My wolf thrashes below the surface, furious that he can't stake a claim on her right here, right now. Furious some other guy is here questioning my right to protect her. I don't touch him—roughing up humans is forbidden—but I shove my chest right into his personal space, getting so close I make him look up into my nostrils.

"Nobody." Lauren tries to insert herself between us.

I shoot an arm out to tuck her safely behind me.

"*Leave it, Oakley.*" Lincoln packs more authority in his tone than I would have thought possible for a human. My body doesn't respond like it would to an actual alpha command, but he wins a grudging respect from me. Especially considering I have at least seventy-five pounds on his tall but lanky form. "My sister doesn't need you to play bodyguard."

Lauren's fingers wrap around my biceps, giving me that sweet hit of candy apple and cinnamon. "I don't."

I don't move. I'm an alpha. There's no fucking way I'll back down to a human, especially not a human pretending he has some claim on Lauren.

"Get in the car, Luke," Lincoln pushes his way between the two of us and gives his friend a shove toward the front of the car. He opens the driver's side door and climbs in.

Pretty boy—Luke, I guess his name is—walks backward, glaring my way. When he tries to see past me to look at Lauren, I shift to block her from his view.

"Lauren, this is fucked up," he shoots across the car as he throws open the passenger side door.

"I...I don't know why you came." The heaviness—the

emptiness—in Lauren's voice drops my aggression level. A vision of her standing on that cliff with one foot over the edge flashes in my mind.

I turn to face her. She releases her grip on my arm and blinks up at me.

I haven't seen this look on her before. It's almost like... she needs something from me. No, that's not it. Because she doesn't appear to know what she wants. It's more like she's lost but hopes I might have something she needs, whatever it is.

It makes me *fucking determined* to figure out what it is and give it to her.

"Let me drive you home," I say gruffly. "Or wherever you want to go." Because I know I may be the last person she wants to be with, I add, "I know a great cliff you could throw me off."

Miraculously, it seems I said the right thing.

Her bare shoulders—her perfect, glorious bare shoulders—relax away from her ears. A reluctant smile tugs at her lips. "Oh yeah?"

The Tesla pulls away without either of us looking at it. Her big teal eyes are on mine.

"Yeah. That sounds good."

I grin back, a spark of lightness I haven't felt in years dancing in my chest. "Which part? Throwing me off a cliff?"

Her smile widens. She's so achingly pretty. I want to eat her up. Devour her. Demolish all the boundaries between us and forever claim her as mine.

Of course, that can't happen.

But I can take care of her tonight.

"Is that a real option?" She lets me touch her, and my

hand settles lightly at her lower back to guide her toward my midnight blue Range Rover.

I shrug. "Sure. Let's do it." I open the door for her, taking a quick look around to make sure no one sees us, but fortunately, by some grace of Fate, there's no one else in the brewery parking lot. There's a security guard at the exit, but he'll be watching people coming in, not going out.

I shrug out of my suit jacket and toss it in the back seat as I climb behind the wheel.

When I pull out of the lot, Lauren leans her head back against the seat and groans.

"Want me to kill him?" I offer. "Please, I'd love to."

"I don't even know what just happened."

I wait. Lauren and I aren't even friends–I have no reason to hope she'll share with me, but, dammit, I need her story. I need to know and understand everything about this enigmatic girl.

My silence works.

"Nothing makes sense to me these days." She looks over at me. "Including you. Although the wolf-thing explained a lot."

I try and fail to swallow. My wolf preens over the knowledge that she's given me thought. That she wants to understand me.

"I haven't told anyone, if that's what this is about."

I clear my throat. "It's not. But thank you."

"Luke and I..."

I grind my teeth to keep from growling at those three words.

"He was there for me when my mom died. So I feel like I owe him some feeling, but I'm just...bone dry. Like crying over my mom. I just can't dredge up anything at all."

I shouldn't celebrate that. I really shouldn't. She's troubled by her lack of sensation.

She sucks in a breath. "But part of me thinks he was just using me for his own social status. I really can't figure out why he came out here, unless it was just to say he was taking me to Homecoming. I tried to break up with him on the phone, and he said I owed it to him to do it in person."

I let out a low growl that snaps Lauren's gaze to me. "Sorry." I clear my throat again. "But you don't owe him jack. He sounds like a prick."

"He's not," she says, but she doesn't sound convinced. After a moment, she says, "Well, maybe he is. But it didn't bother me before. I understood it–maybe I was a prick then, too."

"You said it." I grin, and she whacks my arm with the back of her hand.

"Where are we?"

I've driven up the mountain past my family's cabin. Wilde told me after the first dance that he was taking Rayne up there, and I should keep everyone away until they came out.

I roll to a stop on the side of the dirt road. "The cliff is just a short hike from here."

Lauren looks down at her silver stilettos doubtfully.

"I'll carry you."

"I don't really want to push you off a cliff." She's staring straight ahead, like it would be too much to admit it to my face.

"It wouldn't hurt me, Pearls. If it gets you off, I'm game."

Her lips part in surprise, and she finally meets my gaze. The scent of her arousal blooms, intoxicating and sweet. A choked laugh tumbles from her lips. "It might."

I smile back, that quiver of lightness in my chest again.

"Let's go find out." I push the door open and walk around to her side of the vehicle. She opens the door and unbuckles her seatbelt. Before she can jump down, I pluck her from the Range Rover and toss her over my shoulder.

She shrieks, pounding on my back. "You asshole! Seriously, Abe, are you never not a dick?"

"Never." I jog to the cliff's edge and set her down. "What are you going to do about it, Pearls?" I position myself at the edge of the cliff.

Her eyes widen with excitement, right before she gives my chest a hard shove with both of her palms.

I allow myself to tumble backward off the cliff, then whirl in the air to straighten for the landing. I drop onto my feet, my knees softening to absorb the shock.

There's a breeze cooling the desert air, and I catch the scent of the bear, along with the mingled scents of other wolves—male and female. Wilde, I believe. And the other must be Rayne's. They were out here recently.

"Boo," Lauren cat-calls me from above. "No fair."

I look up and trace the shapely lines of her legs to where they disappear under her skirt. My mouth waters. "Your turn."

"What?"

"You heard me." I hold my arms out. "I'll catch you."

That's all it takes. Apparently, for no conceivable reason, Lauren trusts me. She leaps off the edge of the cliff, the hem of her teal skirt fluttering as she plummets straight down into my arms.

I catch her honeymoon style and swing her around to break the fall. She laughs, and it does something funny to my chest. "God, yes." She drops her head back, her long copper hair cascading toward the ground like a waterfall. "That was exactly what I needed."

"Yeah?" I'm trying to figure her out. I want to get this girl more than I've wanted anything in my life.

"Can I do it again?"

"What am I? An amusement park ride?"

She relaxes in my arms and looks up at the stars. A little smile tugs the corners of her lips, transforming her model-perfect face to something more innocent. Maybe this was how she looked before her mom died. "It's amazing to *feel*," she breathes.

"I'll give you another ride." I put a touch of innuendo in my lowered voice.

I pull the scent of her arousal in through my nostrils, holding my breath like I'm taking a hit from a bong. Not that I partake–it doesn't do much for a shifter. The high only lasts about five minutes. This high will last me all night.

Knowing I'm turning Lauren on. That she wants me.

"I keep thinking about the night with you and the vampire. This is crazy, but...it was the best time I've had in a year. I mean, it sucked, too." She touches the place at her neck where the vampire bit her, and I want to shoot him all over again, even though the mark has already disappeared. "But that adrenaline shocked me back to life." She lifts her head to look at me. "Like watching a horror film, where you're scared, but you also love every minute of it."

An idea starts to form in my mind. A risky, reckless, delicious idea.

I slowly lower her to her feet, keeping an arm behind her back as she finds balance in her stilettos on the rocky terrain.

"You want a thrill, Lauren Sterling?" My voice rasps deeper than normal.

She lifts her beautiful face. There's an openness to her

expression I would battle thousands to be privy to witness. "What do you have in mind, Abe Oakley?"

"You're gonna need a safe word, princess."

* * *

Lauren

I draw in a sharp breath. Abe's words knock me off balance, and I fall against him.

Instead of steadying me, he loops an arm around my back and pulls my body up tight against his. His skin burns hot beneath his button-down, activating every nerve ending in contact with him.

Despite the flush of heat, goosebumps race along my arms. I'm already drunk on the thrill he gave me jumping off the cliff, and now, another hit of dopamine floods my veins.

Safe word. I'll need a safe word.

I'm not sure what he intends, but the desire that jolts through my body is electric. *Hell, yes.* Whatever he's thinking, *I'm in.*

"Arizona!" I blurt.

His smile turns feral. "*Arizona* is your safe word?"

I don't know why I chose it. I guess because there's some magic in the way my mom and grandma used to invoke it. I grew up thinking Arizona was some mystical magical place, not the baked earth and rock mountains of Wolf Ridge. Until I saw a wolf turn into a man right before my eyes last week, I would have argued it's the furthest thing from magical. But now, I'm beginning to wonder–maybe they sensed something special here that I didn't pick up on before.

"*Arizona* means stop," I say, as if I know anything at all about how this works. I mean I've heard of safe words before, but the activities that require them are a little foggy to me.

Abe's eyes glow in the dark. I see his wolf right beneath the surface, and it sends shivers down my entire body.

"I will give you a sixty-second head start." I love the deep rumble of his voice. The way it seems to enter my body and vibrate. "You run, I chase." His voice grows more devious as he speaks. "When I catch you, princess"– he lifts a lock of my hair, letting the curl slide around his finger– "I get to do whatever the fuck I want with you unless I hear that word."

Oh *gawd*. My pelvic floor lifts and squeezes.

My panties soak.

Everything that comes out of Abe Oakley's mouth is pure sin, and I want exactly what he's offering.

I don't wait for him to tell me when to go, I just push away from him and take off running.

"Be careful, Pearls," he calls after me as I stumble in the darkness on my three-inch heels. "Don't hurt yourself before I have the chance to."

I ignore him and keep on running, his words bouncing around the inside of my head. *Don't hurt yourself before I have the chance to.*

He wants to hurt me.

I should find that gross, but instead I find it delicious.

And I am delirious–thrills of anticipation, fear, and lust crash through me like ocean waves as I find my way out of the canyon to a steep hill I can climb.

I hear only one soft foot tread behind me before Abe catches me with an arm around my waist and a hand under my thigh. He lifts me, face to the sky, my pelvis resting on the broad muscled expanse of his shoulder, my feet kicking up toward the stars.

I grip his arm and shriek, laughter clogging my throat. My dress falls down around my waist. Abe runs swiftly up the side of the hill like it's not a steep incline. Like he doesn't have an extra hundred pounds of weight on his shoulder.

When we reach the top, he spin-tosses me in the air and catches me by the waist facing him. It's better than a roller-coaster. So much better. Abe's showing off his strength and prowess while giving me the ride of my life. He walks with me suspended high above his head. My back hits tree bark, and then I'm pinned, my cocktail dress riding up my thighs, my feet dangling above the ground.

I look down at this glorious man-beast, thrilled at his feral intent. He's not looking at my face. He's eye-to-eye with the juncture of my thighs. His nostrils flare–oh God! Didn't he say he could tell when I'm aroused?

Time seems to shimmer and stand still. My body glories in the fact that I'm living. That I feel alive. Lust kicks through my veins. Adrenaline from playing cat and mouse.

And then he strikes–swift and sure. I choke as he opens his mouth, covers my entire pussy with it. The heat of his breath permeates the fabric of my panties. His teeth scrape lightly until they snag on the string of my miniscule panties, and then he tears it with a single snag on his lengthened canine.

I let out a surprised, wanton sound, completely unrecognizable to my own ears. My arousal drips down my inner thigh as I hook my knees over his shoulders. Now that my pussy is bare, he *devours* me. I lose awareness of where my body stops and Abe's mouth begins. He sucks and laps and nips me like a starved man. Like my taste is the only thing keeping him alive. Like bringing me to orgasm is his only mission in life.

This is not the few flicks of a tongue I've experienced before. This is passion and hunger. This is what it is to be consumed. My inner thighs tremble, and I buck against his mouth. I tug his hair with one hand, reaching the other up to steady myself against the tree. Not that I believe Abe would let me fall.

"Yeah..." I mutter, closing my eyes, the tension and need building in my core. "Yeah. Okay. Yeah. There. Right there, Abe. Please..."

I come, my inner walls contracting on air.

Abe continues to lick and suck me through the orgasm. Only when I sag with the aftermath does he release his suction on my flesh. He looks up at me with my juices glossing his lips, his ice-blue wolf eyes bright. "You're going to be doing a lot more begging, Pearls. I'm just getting started."

My laugh is ragged. I'm glorying in the exhilaration and satisfaction of the moment. How changed I feel. So different from the girl who put on this dress to go to a stupid school dance with her ex-boyfriend.

Now I feel so expanded. So much more like me than I've ever felt before.

"Come on, princess." Abe lifts me off the tree to straddle his waist. My ripped panties slide up between us, and he snatches them. "Tell me he didn't see these tonight."

I reach for the panties, but he tucks them in his back pocket, somehow still balancing me on his hip with one arm.

"*Tell me, Pearls,*" he growls.

I don't know why I want to make him suffer. It's unfair after what he just did for me, but our relationship hasn't exactly been full of kindness. "Why? You have no right to be jealous."

A low growl sounds in his throat, and his jaw sets. He starts walking swiftly, carrying me along.

"It's not like you're my boyfriend."

When he doesn't answer, I realize that his jealousy must be genuine. Maybe wolves are extra possessive.

"He didn't." I let him off the hook.

Abe's gait doesn't change. I think I still hear him growling like the wild animal he is.

"We haven't done anything since he arrived. Not even a kiss."

The sound of Abe's footsteps change, and I twist to look over my shoulder to see where we are. He pauses and sniffs the air then pushes open the door to his cabin.

A fresh thrill pumps through me, memory of the last time we were here only adding to my excitement.

He carries me into the kitchen, opens a drawer and pulls out duct tape.

A shock of fear makes me tighten my thighs around his waist. No–not fear. Not really. More trepidation. Or fake fear. Fun fear. The kind you feel right as the scary music builds in a horror movie.

"You liked being tied up last time, didn't you, Pearls?" Abe's voice is deeper than usual. Rougher. His long legs carry us straight into a bedroom without turning on any lights.

He drops me in the center of the bed, shoves my dress up to my waist, and rolls me to my belly.

"What are you–*ack!*" I cry out as he slaps my bare ass.

He delivers a flurry of spanks, alternating right and left side. Each one goes straight to my core. My nerve endings spark. The initial slaps sting and shock me, but heat quickly follows. Pleasure nips on its heels.

"That's for wearing those panties when you were out

with *him*," Abe growls. He spanks me harder, and I list away.

He rolls me back to my back and pushes my thighs wide, climbing up to stand on his knees in front of me. "Give me those wrists."

It's a demand, not an ask.

Funny, but there's no resistance in me to bossy Abe. Not like usual. I lift my wrists, eager for whatever he's planning.

He tugs the end of the duct tape to make a long strip, then tears it and winds it around my wrists. "There." His smile is wicked. "You can still hit me if you want."

Oh God–he winked.

I was unprepared for my body's reaction to a wink from this sexy baller. I practically orgasm right then and there.

But he doesn't notice my reaction–he's already moved on. He has plans, and he's not waiting for my permission. He already made that abundantly clear. I have a safe word I can use if I want it to stop.

He strokes his thumb over my sopping slit, pressing firmly when he gets to my clit, pivoting his hand and sliding two fingers inside me.

I cry out, arching, my internal muscles clenching around his fingers in a mini-orgasm.

"I've been dying to get inside this sweet little pussy of yours."

I'm shaking. My low belly trembles. My inner thighs quake. I'm like the rollercoaster that buzzes and trembles as it climbs to the top, right before it drops into the harrowing pitch and breakneck turns.

Words seem out of reach to me now. All that comes out of my mouth is a series of vowels. "Ahhh...ohhh...ahuh."

Abe slides his fingers in and out of me, gently at first, curling them to stroke my inner wall, then at a fast pump.

"Wait... please!" It's too much. Too much pleasure. Too much to hold onto. I need to let go. I kick at him with my spiky heels. He catches one ankle and holds it high while continuing to finger-fuck me.

"Oh my God. Oh my God! Oh please!" My orgasm comes on so hard and fast I shriek. Moisture gushes around Abe's fingers.

"That's it, Pearls," Abe praises me. "Good girl."

"Oh my God. What just happened? What did you do to me?"

"I made you squirt." He looks proud of himself as he eases his fingers out of me and unbuckles the strap on my Jimmy Choo.

Squirt. Female ejaculation. Another term—like *safe word*—I've heard but had no actual understanding of before tonight.

He tosses the heel behind him and unbuckles the other one. "That was your pleasure," he tells me. "Now it's time for punishment."

Chapter Fifteen

*be

My cock is harder than marble. The only thing keeping my wolf sane is the knowledge that I've made Lauren orgasm twice already. Her scent is everywhere—on my clothes, my skin, filling the room.

Wilde and Rayne were here before us—I can tell by their scents—but they're gone now. Probably up on the mesa where the shifter kids all go to hang out around a fire. Where my buddies will be now, wondering where I went.

I picked a different bedroom, so I can indulge only in Lauren's scent.

It brings massive satisfaction. Having the taste of her on my lips and fingers takes the edge off my aggression as well.

But, damn, the urge to mark her keeps riding up my back, constricting the nerves at the base of my skull that allow me to see straight. But it doesn't matter. I don't need to see to make Lauren come. I don't need to see to make her scream and beg and writhe on the bed. At this point, if you told me I'd never see again, I'm not sure I would care. Because pleasuring Lauren is my life purpose.

Lauren's eyes are glassy, her thick mane of coppery hair spreads out around her face like a halo. I blink to bring her into better focus. She's a fucking goddess. I don't care if my physiology is screwed up, and that's why my wolf wants to mark a human. It feels so right. The satisfaction of being with her can't be wrong.

"You liked that spanking I gave you, didn't you, Pearls?"

She rubs her pouty lips together. "Uh—I don't know about that."

"Liar." I know by the fresh bloom of her arousal that I'm right. I run my index finger through her juices, then hold it up to show her. "Your body tells me everything." I bring it to my mouth to taste, and my vision goes dark, temples throbbing.

I roll her over, so she won't see, in case anything shows on my face. "I'm adding lying to the list of punishable offenses." I grab a pillow to thrust under her hips, and my vision clears. Her skin still shows my handprints from before, a reminder that she's a delicate human. I slap her ass and squeeze it. "You have the best ass, princess. Full and round and fucking perfect." I slap the other side. "This ass has been *a torment* to me since the day you walked into Chemistry and ruined my life." I deliver a flurry of rapid slaps, then stop and rub her soft flesh, soothing it. Worshiping it.

I pry her cheeks apart and look at her cute asshole. "Next time I'm going to fuck you right here." I press my thumb against her little rosebud, and she squeezes against it. "And you're going to tell me you're sorry."

"What makes you think there will be a next time?" Lauren tosses her hair when she turns to look over her shoulder at me, resting up on her forearms.

I give her my cockiest smile. "Oh, there will be a next

time." I deliver another flurry of smacks, and she shrieks, laughing and listing away.

There *has* to be a next time. Now that I've tasted her, I'm addicted. I won't be able to function if I can't get her under my hands and tongue on a regular basis.

I continue with my game–slapping her, rubbing away the sting, spanking again, until she's dripping with arousal, moaning with need. I pull the pillow out and roll her back onto her back then do what I should have done the moment I got her in here–I pull her slinky dress off over her head. It's strapless–thank fate–so it doesn't get hung up on her bound hands. She sits up to help me, and I toss it to the floor with the shoes.

"Oh, sweet moon goddess," I breathe, staring at her tits. She has flower stickers or something over each of her nipples. A surge of jealousy rips through me. "Did you put those on *for him?*" My voice cracks like I'm twelve. I rub my temples, trying to keep my vision from glitching.

"No. You're being ridiculous." Lauren appears amused at my jealousy.

I exhale through my teeth.

"They're to keep my nipples from showing through the dress." She tries to reach one of them with her fingertips but can't with the duct tape. "Peel them off."

Aw, damn. A sense of possessiveness overtakes the jealousy. I get to be the one to take them off her.

Because she's mine, my wolf snarls.

Yeah, down boy.

My cock surges against my zipper. I catch Lauren's wrists and use them to nudge her backward until she's lying flat, then I climb over her. The nipple covers are slightly padded, like little gelatinous flower petals. I peel the edge of one of them up. It's stuck on with some kind of adhesive. "Does that hurt?" I ask, watching her skin lift with it.

"Do it fast."

I rip it off quick, watching her breast lift and then spring back. I swirl my tongue over her nipple to soothe away the sting then repeat the action on the other side.

"Glorious fucking breasts," I murmur against her skin. I could lick every inch of her body and still need to taste more.

"I'm going to fuck you now, Pearls." I watch her face closely to see her reaction.

I know now that Lauren fronts as much as an alpha wolf. She may act mature and sexualized, but who knows? She could still be a virgin. I don't want to blow past her boundaries because we're playing some hunter and prey game.

"Make it good."

Make. It. Good. That's my princess. I fucking love this girl. I love every detestable, delicious, perfect thing about her.

"If good means *fuck you hard without mercy*, then, yeah. I'm gonna make it good." I can front, too.

She arches those beautiful tits up toward my face, and I grip one breast roughly and squeeze, a low growl rumbling in my chest.

"Show me, wolf-boy."

I unbuckle my belt. "Oh I'm no boy, princess. I'm about to show you that I'm" –I unzip my suit trousers– *"all man."*

The tip of Lauren's pink tongue rims her lips as I free my erection. I nearly come from the thought of seeing that mouth stretched wide, choking on my cock.

I back off the bed to kick off my shoes and strip. "I have a condom," I tell her, fishing it out of my wallet.

"I'm on the pill."

My wolf snarls at the idea of her having sex with *him*. With anyone before me.

"Does that make you jealous, too?"

I must've snarled out loud. Fortunately, she still sounds amused by my irrational possessiveness.

"I'm about to fuck him out of your memory bank, sweetheart." I climb over her and roll the condom over my member.

"Cocky, much?" Her eyes are on my dick, her lips open.

I haven't even kissed those lips yet. A problem I need to remedy immediately.

"Every minute of the day." I slowly drag the head of my cock over her slit.

She sucks in a breath and holds it.

I continue to rub the head of my cock through her juices. "Do you want this cock, Pearls?"

Her lids droop, but she doesn't answer. But then, we're playing at non-consent, so maybe answering would spoil the game.

Despite my big talk, I ease into her gently, making sure she's ready for it, and it's not too much. I know I'm big, and I don't know how much experience she has. I definitely don't want to do anything that doesn't satisfy her.

As soon as I'm inside her, I set up a slow rhythm and lean over to claim that mouth. She watches as I lower my head, and then her eyes flutter closed when my lips brush hers. As I kiss her, I take her wrists and slowly raise them over her head, so she's pinioned beneath me.

She starts to writhe, as if being held down turns her on. I tighten my grip and thrust a little harder. Our tongues dance and tangle. Her kiss is everything, and my control slips. It feels so good–so right–to claim that pouty mouth of hers. I kiss her like I mean it—like she belongs to me, belongs under me, over me, with me, every second of the day.

I finally have her where I want her, and I still crave more. I crave all of her—heart, mind, soul. Not just this hot little body that responds like it was made for me. Like I was made for her.

Lauren starts to pant and make these sweet little moaning sounds as she grinds up to meet me. I thrust harder, unable to hold back any longer. This has been far too long in coming. I may be a premiere athlete, but this girl is always my undoing.

"Aw, fuck, Lauren," I growl. "I can't...it's too much—"

She hooks her ankles behind my back and uses her legs to pull me in even harder. "Do it," she snarls, no less alpha than any she-wolf I've been with.

I shout, my balls drawing up tight just before I crest the peak.

"Fuuuuuck! Oh, Fate. Oh, fuck." I lick my thumb and reach down to rub her clit right before I come harder than I've ever come. Lauren bucks beneath me, her inner thighs squeezing my hips like a vise, her sweet pussy contracting and releasing around my cock.

She's still coming when I finish, her eyes rolled back, her chin jutting up toward the ceiling, those gorgeous breasts lifted and spread. As I look down at her I know with all certainty that having Lauren Sterling isn't some itch I can scratch and get over.

Deny it all I want, but this girl is my destiny. And now that I've had her, nothing will ever be the same.

* * *

Lauren

I'm officially alive. Not just alive–flying. It's like Abe just put the shock paddles to my chest and brought me back from the dead.

When my eyes flutter open, I find Abe staring down at me with an intensity that brings on another mini-orgasm.

He's just watching like I'm the most fascinating thing on Earth. I'm used to attention, but not from Abe. He comes off as all about himself. But then, that might just be part of his alpha persona–the one he wears at school. He's actually shown himself to be considerate on more than one occasion.

He lowers his mouth to mine again, slowly pumping into me, wringing out more little squeezes and ripples of pleasure. His kiss is attentive this time. Where before he was feral, now he's suave. He licks into my lips, then backs away, then approaches again.

"Are you okay? Was I too rough?" he asks, still moving slowly inside me.

I can barely think. I'm not sure I'm verbal yet. Does he expect a real answer?

"M'good," I manage to say. "So good."

He pulls back a little more to see my face and gives me the most beautiful boyish grin. "Yeah?"

My lids droop with the continued pleasure he's giving me. "Don't get cocky."

"Cocky is my middle name."

"I've noticed." I reach up, wanting to touch him back. My wrists are still bound with duct tape, but I trace my fingertips over his lips.

He nips at them, sucking one into his mouth, then releasing it.

"It's an alpha wolf thing, right? The swagger?"

Abe blinks, and for a moment, I see a crack in his

facade–like something about my question momentarily pained him.

"What is it?" My voice is soft, not like the usual challenges I hurl at him.

"Eh." He pulls out, and I'm instantly sorry I asked. Sorry I pushed on his sore spot. I already miss the connection of our bodies. Our souls. He climbs off the bed and disposes of the condom then returns with a glass of water. He lifts under my shoulders to hold me up to drink.

I'm not used to intimacy like this. Being helpless to Abe, but also being under his protection is a flavor I've never experienced before. I love how easily he lifts and positions me, how he takes ownership of my pleasure.

I drink the water down, thirstier than I knew, studying Abe as I do.

"Heavy is the crown that rules Wolf Ridge High?" I ask when he takes the glass away.

One corner of his lips lifts in a wry grin. "I guess. To be honest, there's absolutely no pleasure in it."

"Then why maintain it? What's the reward? Kids doing your work and sucking up to you but not actually liking you?" Abe's expression shutters, and I realize I'm biting too hard. I reach out and grab his forearm with my bound hands. "I'm sorry. That was mean. I really do want to know. Because I feel like that's not the real you."

Longing pierces Abe's gaze. He stares at me like I'm offering something he can't have. The air between us charges. I hold my breath, waiting for...whatever Abe's inner struggle is.

But he seems to shake himself then drops his gaze to my hands. In one deft rip, he busts through the layers of tape to free my wrists. "Who do you think the real me is?" There's a bitterness to his tone that twists like a blade in my belly.

It feels vulnerable when most of our interactions have been snarking at each other, but I say, "This. Right now."

Some kind of shock visibly runs through Abe's body–a shudder of recognition? Instead of speaking, he reaches for my face, cradling it as he kisses the hell out of me.

I moan against his lips, hot tears suddenly burning the backs of my eyes. I have no idea what they mean.

Who they're for.

For Abe? The lost and lonely alpha wolf? Or for me? The girl who couldn't cry?

No...it's more about the beauty of the moment. Finding someone to share the broken pieces of our lives.

When he breaks the kiss, a tear spills from one of my eyes. Abe sucks in a breath, bringing the pad of his thumb to my cheek to catch it. "Did I make you feel again?" His voice sounds rusty.

I nod. "Yeah," I whisper.

"This is the real me." He sprawls his long form beside mine and wraps his arm around my waist, drawing me against his heated skin.

I touch his chest, running my nails through the soft golden curls there. Another ripple runs through him at my touch, and his eyes glow in the darkness.

"My dad..." He clears his throat. "It's important to my dad that I maintain alpha status."

"Why?"

Abe gives an impatient shake of his head. "It's a family thing. He's unrelenting about it. He has been ever since the Change when I became my wolf. Before then, I felt like I had my whole life ahead of me, like my future was open and expansive. And now...now it's like I'm locked into a mold I don't even fit. Nothing is fun anymore. Even my interactions with my best friends feel fake."

I stare at Abe, shocked by his admission. It doesn't make sense to me, but I'm not a wolf. Maybe it's some cultural thing I don't get.

"What would happen if you didn't play the part?"

"I don't know. I'd lose my status. Someone else would take Alpha–probably Asher. Markley's stronger, but Asher's got a desperate streak. His dad got kicked out of the pack."

"I mean with your dad."

Abe scrubs a hand across his face. "I don't want to disappoint him. He wants what's best for me and our family line. My brother did everything my dad wanted him to. He's the pre-med golden boy, following in Dad's footsteps, and I'm a fuck-up."

I scoff. "Is that what you think? You're the captain of the football team. The alpha wolf of the whole school. How can you possibly think of yourself as a fuck-up?" And then I remember his struggle to perform in the lab. "Is this about schoolwork?"

Abe doesn't answer.

"Abe..." I hesitate because my question is going to poke at his high alphaness. "Has anyone ever tested you for neurodivergence? Or have you had your eyesight tested? Sometimes it seems like you have trouble seeing or reading. I wondered if you could be dyslexic or something."

I realize Abe isn't breathing at all. "I can't believe—" he chokes. "How did you figure that out?"

"What is it? Neurodivergence?"

He sits up in the bed. "You can't tell anyone, Lauren. This is the whole reason I have to maintain alpha status."

I sit up, too, stroking my palm over his bulging biceps. My heart thuds with the magnitude of the moment. Abe's walls coming down. His secrets revealed. "I won't tell anyone. But what is it, Abe?" I ask softly.

"It's a genetic defect–shifter related. My brain sometimes glitches on whether I'm seeing with my wolf eyes or my human eyes. It gives me headaches and makes it hard to read. The fluorescent lights make it worse."

"Oh, wow."

"I was managing it, totally hiding the condition until this year."

"What happened this year?"

When Abe turns to look at me, something makes the hairs on my arms stand up. The air turns electric.

Abe's eyes glow ice blue.

"*You* happened, princess."

Chapter Sixteen

Abe

Lauren reaches over and turns on a bedside lamp. It's not even a fluorescent light, but still, my eyes react. Pain shoots diagonally through my visual field, and the muscles contract the base of my skull.

"Is it happening now?" Lauren is so attuned to me, she somehow knows.

My instinct is to lie, to go on the offensive to distract attention from myself, as I've been doing with everyone else, but something won't let me. "Yeah," I croak.

My visual field has constricted so tightly that I can't see anything, but Lauren slides her hands over my bare shoulders.

My cock gets semi-hard again.

"I make it worse?"

"Yeah," I admit. My secret's already out. "Your scent triggers it."

"That's why you've been such a dick to me." She doesn't sound upset about it, more thoughtful.

There's so much more beneath Lauren Sterling's exterior. She's smart, perceptive, and actually caring. For some reason, knowing that makes my chest constrict.

This thing between us is going beyond lust. Beyond her scent sparking a physical attraction. There's an unexpected emotional connection—a genuine one.

I may actually be falling for this girl. She's becoming more than just a pheromone-directed crush. She could be a *true* mate—like in the human sense of the word.

A soul mate.

I lift her, my hands spanning her slender waist, and settle her on my lap, straddling my legs. "I'm sorry I was a dick."

She's still studying me. "It wasn't real." It's not a question. She's decided it for herself.

I give a weary shrug. "I don't even know what's real, Lauren. Who I am or who I'm supposed to be. I'm just trying to get by each day without losing control."

She cups my face between her hands, and my belly shudders in at the tenderness of it. The pain behind my eyes ceases. The episode is past.

When she slants her mouth over mine, I suddenly believe I could be made whole again.

Not that I'd even been aware of how broken I was before this moment.

I don't take over, I allow her soft, exploratory kiss. Her healing kiss.

"This is who you are," she murmurs when she breaks it.

I fill my hands with her ass and yank her over my hardened cock. "What about you? Is this who you are?"

Lauren rocks her hips, rubbing her clit over my root. Her lips hover and dance over mine. "No."

I try not to show the savagery her answer inspires. My wolf thrashes jealously beneath the surface.

"This is...something new. What I am with you is completely different."

I barely remember to breathe. "Different, how?"

She tilts her head to the side, considering. "I hardly remember who I was before my mom died, but that girl is never coming back. And for the last year, I've been...flat. The only time I felt real emotion was when my dad attempted suicide, and that was complete despair."

I suck in a breath like she punched me. "Your dad attempted suicide?" Fuck. That selfish prick. He has two kids who fucking need him.

Her chin wobbles, and she blinks rapidly. "There you go again. You're the only one who can make me cry."

I wrap my arms tightly around her and draw her against my chest in a fierce hug. "I'm sorry, princess," I whisper. "I'm so fucking sorry."

"That's why we moved to Arizona. My mom loved it here. My dad had that house built for her, but she didn't live long enough to enjoy it. Lincoln and I hoped living here would help him feel closer to her. Plus, we'd be able to leave the emptiness of our old lives behind."

My lips find the hollow of her throat, and I kiss it. "I had it so wrong. I thought you two were stuck up rich kids who thought you were better than us."

Lauren lets out a mirthless chuff. "Well, that might have been true. But mostly we don't care about or want to have a social life here. Our job is to keep a close eye on our dad. Keeping him alive is our only goal this year."

My eyes burn for a moment.

Fuck. I want to howl at the moon goddess for the cards Lauren and Lincoln were dealt. I want to dedicate my entire life to standing guard over their dad, so she can go back to living. I want to be her hero—to vow to keep the one parent she has left safe for her.

I kiss down her neck. Along her jaw. "I'm so sorry," I murmur.

My words don't help anything, and I fucking hate feeling helpless. "What can I do to help?"

Lauren burrows her fingertips through my hair, and my entire body shudders with the pleasure of it. "You have helped. That day a ghost-eyed wolf charged me at the edge of a cliff changed my life. It was like you put jumper paddles to my chest. Life went from black and white to color again. Only the colors are far more rich than I ever noticed before."

Intensity plows through me. Without thinking, I throw Lauren to her back. I'm already pushing inside her when I realized my canines have descended. My wolf wants to mark her as my mate, right here, right now.

It's not happening. It can't.

But I'm powerless to stop the pure animal-like instinct to claim her. It's a good thing she's on the pill because I didn't stop to put on a condom.

Lauren's gaze is startled pleasure. Her lips—puffy from our kisses—part with a moan.

Too late, I check for permission—in the pretend-forced way she likes it. "I'm gonna fuck you so hard, princess, you'll never go numb again."

She reaches for my hips, lifting her knees up to take me deeper. "Do it, wolf-boy."

"Not a boy." I hold her shoulders down to pin her in place and pump in deep, bottoming out against her inner walls.

Her cries grow louder. More agitated.

"Lauren...Lauren," I chant her name, not sure what I'm

even saying. Like she's a goddess I'm invoking rather than a slip of a human I'm in danger of splitting in two with the force of this fucking.

Don't mark her. Don't mark her, I remind myself.

To slow down, I dive onto my back, keeping our bodies connected, so she can ride me now. I grip her hips and do the work for her, lifting her up and down over my rock-hard cock, then forward and back.

She throws her head back, her long coppery hair shimmering in the lamplight. Her ripe breasts shift with each bounce.

"Beautiful," I growl. "Beautiful little human. You drive me fucking mad."

Her gaze returns from the ceiling to my face. "Do I?" There's an interesting, almost shifter-like glint of light to her eyes. They've darkened. Rounded. Like she loves knowing she has power over me.

She's all goddess again. The powerful, beautiful female responsible for my daily torture.

I'm blinded again, my eye muscles burning through my skull.

"Insane," I mutter. I'm incapable of denying it. Incapable of denying her anything.

"Abe." Her hand cradles the side of my face, and the pain immediately dissipates. "Can you see?"

I blink and nod. "I see you. Always you."

She rocks over me, slowly now. Undulating like a belly dancer.

I watch, transfixed. She squeezes her own breasts, rolls her hips. Then she finds a rhythm she likes. A place where the head of my cock rolls over an inner ridge inside her. She rubs faster. Braces her hands on my shoulders to go at it. I help, urging her hips forward with my hands on her ass.

Her internal muscles squeeze around my cock. Her inner thighs shake against my hips. She cries out–no, screams–as she comes. She holds still, squeezing and releasing around my cock. Then rocks a little and comes some more.

I wet the pad of my thumb with my tongue and bring it to her clit. When I rub, she screams again, bucking and squeezing in a complete loss of control.

The moment she's done, I throw her to her back and pound into her. My canines are long, but I keep my mouth closed, keep my torso upright, so I won't lean over and sink my teeth into her flesh to forever mark her.

I slam into her, harder than I should. I have to hold her shoulder to keep her head from smashing into the head-board. She whines and mewls beneath me. It's too much–I know it is–but I can't dial back my aggression. Can't slow down.

Only Lauren could stop me now, and she's as far in the throes as I am.

I close my eyes as lightning streaks across my vision.

"Fuck...yes!" I shout. The pain in my head intensifies, but I don't care. I come. I come, and I come inside her right before I black out entirely.

* * *

Lauren

Abe's eyelids flicker when he comes, and then–suddenly–he's on top of me, his heavy body covering mine like one of those weighted blankets.

I panic at first, trying to push 200 plus pounds of solid muscle off, so I can see his face and make sure he's okay.

I can't budge him from me at all, but I feel the movement of his breath against my chest.

"Abe?" I force myself to remain calm and lightly stroke the back of his neck with my fingertips.

He jerks and shakes himself, as if startled awake, and pushes up on his hands, easing out of me. "Oh fuck, Lauren, are you all right?"

I let out a relieved laugh. "Me?"

"What happened?" Abe looks shaken. "I didn't bite you, did I?"

"Bite me?" Now that he says it, I remember thinking his teeth looked particularly wolf-like when he came. Not creepy, like that vampire's, but very canine-like. "No. Why would you bite me?"

He shakes his head.

Outside, in the distance, a wolf howls. Then others join it, rising to a crescendo like a pack celebrating a fresh kill.

"Friends of yours?" I ask.

"Definitely." He backs off the bed and holds his hand out. When I take it, he tugs me off the bed. "We should get out of here in case they come around."

I'm too blissed out from the incredible orgasms and the closeness I feel to Abe to pay much attention to the sliver of unease that sprouts about his desire to hide me from his friends.

I'm not a wolf shifter–I get it. And I know he's a wolf. If that got out, he'd be in trouble, and I'd get mind-wiped.

But I'm not used to being someone's shameful secret, either. I'm used to being the prize.

I forget it all when Abe slides my dress over my head. It's kinda sexy to be dressed like a Barbie doll by your boyfriend.

Er–I guess he's not my boyfriend, but whatever. It's still hot.

Abe smoothes the dress down, sliding his large palms down my sides, around to my ass, where he squeezes. "Do you feel better, Princess?" His voice is low and bedroom-y.

I bring my hands to his sculpted chest, my fingertips tracing the lines of his pecs. "Yeah." Of course, I have to go home to the mess I made with Luke, but that's on me.

"I can meet you here any evening or night after practice and give you what you need. Even if it's just another toss off a cliff."

A laugh tumbles out of me. Warmth curls in my chest, filling the places that went cold when we heard the wolves. "I might take you up on that, baller."

"Might?" He sounds offended.

I laugh again. "Okay, I will. Probably."

"Pearls, you are the hardest to get of all hard-to-gets."

"When did you ever make any attempt to get me?" I shoot back.

He grins. "Oh yeah. That's fair." He grabs his clothes and pulls them on, then yanks the bedding from the bed and carries it out.

"That's very responsible of you." I don't know why seeing Abe do this little piece of domesticity is a turn-on.

"Wolves can smell everything." He stuffs the sheets into a washing machine and pours the liquid soap in. "My parents totally know that me and my friends use this cabin– that's what it's for, really–but I don't need them to know everything." He gives me a boyish grin with a waggle of his brows that turns me to soft goo. I love this side of Abe.

The *real* side. The ordinary-extraordinary young man who washes sheets and tries to be a good son to his parents.

The guy who I know now struggles with a neural condition that he works very hard to hide. Not for himself, but for his father.

My heart—which had been barely beating before—has now come back to a steady rhythm, and it's pulsing in perfect time with Abe's.

He starts the washer and stalks to the kitchen. "You hungry?"

"I thought you were trying to get me out of here."

"I am, but I'm also starving. Being with you is a huge calorie-drain." He opens the refrigerator and pulls out a carton of milk, which he opens and chugs.

"Because I trigger your neural thing?" There's something I still don't understand about that. Why would my scent be any different for him? Why do *I* set him off?

He meets my eyes over the top of the milk carton. In the light of the refrigerator door, they take on that ice-blue glow. "Something like that," he says after he finishes gulping down the entire container.

He tosses it in the trash.

"Who keeps this place stocked with food?" I ask.

"My mom, I guess. She knows how hungry growing wolves can get after shifting."

Loss engulfs me. The pain of not having a mom to do those little things—to make sure I've eaten enough or ask about homework or any of the other little things moms do—hits me so hard, I sway on my feet. "That's sweet," I manage to choke out. "Moms are...amazing."

Abe must hear something in my voice because I'm instantly crushed against his chest. "Fuck, Pearls. I'm sorry."

I soak up the embrace. I've been pushing people away for over a year. Not wanting touch. But now that I'm cracked open, now that I feel again, it's incredible to be held.

It's also just incredible to experience this pain. This grief. This loss that I held at bay for so long.

Rather than fight it, I lean into it. Let it soak through me. No, that's not right–it's coming from the inside out. I'm emitting pain.

And the pain is wonderful. Because it's me. It's mine. I'm alive and in pain and actually grieving the loss of my mom.

"No, it's good. I'm finally feeling it. God, for so long, I thought I was broken. Possibly a horrible daughter. Now I know I was just in an emotional coma or something." I pull back and look up at Abe.

He cradles my face in his large hands and leans down to put his forehead against mine. "You're not broken." He murmurs the words, his breath feathering across my lips. "You're perfect as you are, Lauren Sterling." He brushes his lips over mine, then kisses each of my cheeks and my forehead. "The way you grieve or don't grieve is your own. It's not right or wrong. It can be in your own time. It seems to me like you had to hit pause on grieving because your dad was a selfish bastard and tried to kill himself."

A gully opens up right in the middle of my chest. The enormity of our father's suicide attempt–the terror it provoked in me that I might lose both parents–hits me, threatening to swallow me like a sink-hole. I cling to Abe to stay present. To not disappear again.

"You're not broken," Abe murmurs again. "Do you still believe that?"

"When I'm with you, it feels like I could climb out of the wreckage. Like I've been in a car accident, and I hit my head. I dreamed the last year away. And now, suddenly, I'm awake. I can see that I'm still trapped in the broken pieces and parts, but I could climb out."

Abe slides his hand to the back of my head and grips my hair, surprising me with his change from tender to masterful. He lowers his lips to my ear. "When you say things like that, I want to fucking *consume you*," he growls.

He pulls away, and his canines glint in the moonlight coming through the window.

A shudder of recognition goes through me although I don't know what I'm recognizing. My body reacts with a flush of heat. A clenching between my legs. A thrumming need to return to that bedroom.

Wolf-yips sound from a different direction this time.

"Fuck," Abe mutters, taking my hand. "I need to get you home."

Chapter Seventeen

Lauren

I wake up late and roll out of bed. My body is sore in all the right places, and I'm surprised to feel a little zip in my step, like the awakening I experienced with Abe last night is still present. I feel alive, even after the adrenaline rush of jumping off a cliff and being chased and tied up by a hot guy has worn off.

If I was feeling guilty about being out with Abe after the way Luke and I left things, it dissolved when I came home last night and realized Lincoln and Luke weren't even home yet. Apparently, they found a great party in Tempe and stayed for it.

After a long shower, I dress and head into the kitchen. My dad sits at the table by the wall of windows that overlook the mountainside. He's still in a bathrobe, despite it being close to noon.

I kiss his temple. "You're not dressed."

We had an agreement–he's supposed to take care of himself, which includes showering and eating.

"It's a weekend."

"True." I pour myself a bowl of Golden Grahams and sit down across the table from him.

"I saw a bear this morning."

"You did?" My skin prickles. Are there bear shifters? Is that another species in Wolf Ridge that I didn't know about?

Nah, probably not. I remind myself to ask Abe.

I have so many burning questions for him. Last night he put his number in my phone, so I could tell him when I wanted to throw him off a cliff again. I feel that little pop and fizz of excitement when I think about texting him later about the bear. Or about seeing him again.

"It looked like a grizzly, but that seems unlikely. I was reading up on it. Grizzlies used to be native to the Grand Canyon area, but they're now endangered, and Arizona hasn't made a plan for reintroduction. In fact, the state was being sued by the Arizona Center for Biological Diversity for not putting a plan in place."

I gape at my father. It's the first time he's taken an interest in anything in longer than I can remember.

"Oh wow. That would be cool if we had the only grizzly in Arizona wandering around Moongaze Hill."

One corner of my dad's mouth lifts. "Your mom would love that. She had a thing for bears."

"She did? How did I not know that?" That information slices me open. This feeling thing has its drawbacks.

But no—I want to feel. I want the pain of losing my mom to be present. At least I know I'm alive and caring.

"Oh yes. We took a trip to Alaska once, and she was so excited to see bears in the wild. It gave her such a thrill. I think it had something to do with Grandma. She loved bears, too."

"Did she see one in the Grand Canyon?"

Supposedly, my mom's love for Arizona came from

Grandma, who took a wild road trip to the Grand Canyon with her college friends in a convertible Volkswagen after graduation in the seventies.

Grandma had never gone back, but she made Mom promise to go and see the Grand Canyon when she was dying of breast cancer. Yes—the same cancer that killed Mom fifteen years later.

"Your grandma? I have no idea," my dad says. "But your mom said she used to spend the entire visit to the Bronx Zoo in front of the bear exhibit ranting about how bears shouldn't be kept in enclosures."

"Oh yeah. Mom used to say that, too," I remember. The pang of not knowing her morphs into something warmer. Like talking about Mom brings that sense of being loved by her back.

My dad turns his gaze from the window to me. "How was Homecoming?"

"Um...well, Luke and I broke up, but I hung out with another guy, so it ended up okay."

My dad blinks. "You and Luke broke up...I'm sorry, hon. I didn't even know that was coming."

"Yeah, that's okay."

"Should I have known?"

"Well, he came out so we could break up in person, which didn't make sense to me, but what do I know?"

I expected him to be disappointed, since he's buddies with Luke's dad, but he just looks at me thoughtfully. "I never really thought you two fit," he says.

"You didn't?"

He shakes his head. "No. I felt like he was riding your coattails. He liked your social status and took advantage of your need for a friend while your mom was dying."

My eyes burn, and I blink quickly at my cereal. I don't

think I realized until this moment how little my dad has been attending to my life. He was so wrapped up in his own grief he had nothing left to offer me.

Now, just to hear his simple observation about my relationship makes me want to cry like a baby.

He reaches across and covers my hand. "Are you okay?"

I swallow down the lump in my throat. "Yeah." I sniff. The lightness of my recent activities brings a sense of fullness to my heart. "I am okay."

My old life is definitely dead. Whoever I used to be, whatever Luke was or wasn't to me, seems irrelevant.

I am a new person now. Maybe I'm not living vibrantly yet, but I'm coming alive. I turned an enemy into a lover. Jumped off a cliff. Found out vampires and wolf shifters exist.

I hear the shower start up in the hall bathroom. Luke is awake.

I can stop avoiding him. We had it out last night, and we're over. I'm grateful to him for the support he was when my mom was dying, but that's all. The rest is for the past.

This afternoon, I will drive him to the airport and say my goodbyes. Goodbye to Luke. Goodbye to my old life.

I pick up my phone and text Abe. ***Is there such a thing as a bear shifter?***

* * *

Abe

"Where are you going?" my dad demands when I try to slip by the parents with a breezy "see you later."

"For a run—a four-legged one. I have some pent-up aggression to burn off."

Always better to stick close to the truth when you're hiding something. And the pent-up aggression is no lie.

I blacked out again this afternoon when I read Lauren's text saying she was driving Luke to the airport.

Can't Lincoln take him? I almost wrote back, but fortunately, the blackout stopped me from sending it.

Lauren's not even my girlfriend. I don't have a claim on her.

Bullshit, my wolf growls every time I think that.

So now I need to see her—to fuck his memory out of her. Not that she's agreed to this meeting.

I have another reason for defying my alpha and going to her property. She told me her dad saw a bear there. I need to sniff around to see if it was that same old shifter.

"Abe, have you been having any more headaches or visual disturbances this week?"

I hesitate. I don't want to be subjected to more tests. "No. All good. Just aggression."

"You should be channeling that aggression into football, son. Coach Jamison told me the ASU recruiter will be up to watch the game this week. You need to be at your peak performance to get that full ride scholarship we're talking about."

"Yes, sir. I will be."

"I don't see how going for a run at nine at night on a Sunday is compatible prep for the recruiter."

My vision starts going haywire. My wolf wants to come out and tear a piece of my dad's flank right now for trying to keep me from Lauren.

Like always, I cover with bluster. I slam my open hand against the wall making a loud but harmless thud. "I'm letting off steam, so I *can* focus on my game, Dad."

My mom comes in from the family room. "Paul. He's an adult now. Let him make his own choices."

My dad looks troubled. "Fine. But stay away from Moongaze Hill."

Uh, right. "Yep," I say. Another direct order I'll be disobeying.

I jog out of the house and drive my car up toward the cabin then pull over and run the rest of the way to Lauren's in human form. I stop before the clearing to take in the scents. It would be easier to detect the bear's trail in wolf form, but I can't crawl through Lauren's window as a wolf, and I am definitely planning on crawling through that window.

I catch his scent around the perimeter of the Sterling property. It's definitely the old shifter again. The pack's theory that he's selling out young shifters proved wrong. No one's saying much, but I understand Rayne was abducted by a human, and she shifted for the first time to protect herself.

Why is the bear trespassing on pack property, though? Has he gone senile?

I catch movement in Lauren's room, and I leave my musings about the bear. Tomorrow, I'll tell my dad I caught his scent again on pack land.

Right now, I have a beautiful human to torture.

I stay in the shadows and out of the sight-lines of the windows to approach the mansion then hug the side of the house until I'm standing below Lauren's window. When I pry the screen off the frame it hits the window, and I freeze, praying Lauren's dad doesn't come out with his shotgun.

The window flies open. "Seriously?" Lauren whispers, but a beautiful smile lights her face. It takes my breath away.

She's so changed from the haughty rich girl who started at Wolf Ridge High in August.

I take advantage of the open window and throw a hand across the frame to hoist myself up with one arm.

"Show off," she whispers when I swing a leg over and drop onto her hardwood floor. She's wearing a thin pair of blue pajama shorts and a spaghetti strap top that I can't wait to tear off.

I cover her mouth, backing her up until her legs hit the bed. Then I pick her up by the waist and toss her into the center of it.

She lets out a breathy, silent laugh. "What are you doing?"

I pull my shirt off over my head, getting dizzy with lust when Lauren's gaze tracks to my chest and stays there. I kick off my sneakers and climb over her. "What's your safe word?" I breathe, catching her wrists and pinning them down beside her head.

I can't get enough of the light in her eyes.

"Arizona."

I nod. "So, if I hear Arizona, I'm gonna stop. Otherwise, you're at my mercy."

I release her wrists to yank her shorts down. She's not wearing panties underneath, and she's freshly shaven. I nearly jizz in my pants when she reaches down to stroke between her legs. The scent of her arousal fills my nostrils.

"Huh uh." I catch her wrist and pull her hand away, even though her self-pleasure is hot as hell. "I'm doing the pleasuring." I push her knees wide and lick into her.

She jolts, one leg kicking, her hands flying to my head.

I hold both her wrists down by her sides and continue with my tongue, tracing inside her labia, then penetrating her with my stiffened tongue.

She puts her knees over my shoulders, rocking her pelvis to press into my mouth. I suck her, nip, find her clit and flick my tongue over it.

Her breath quickens. She bites her lips, holding in a moan.

I don't let her come. I nibble and lick my way north, sliding her top off as I go and kissing the flat plane of her belly. I lick and suck one nipple as I cup her other breast.

"Take off your top," I command.

I have no idea whether she'll obey or not. I know she likes being forced. I'm not sure whether obedience is her kink.

She holds my gaze as she pulls off her top.

My vision starts going on the fritz. I blink, forcing myself to take a slow breath, and it clears. I find Lauren's brows drawn in concern.

I give a quick shake of my head. "Turn over, Princess, I'm gonna fuck you from behind."

Lauren doesn't obey this time. I'm ready to dial it back when she says, "Make me."

I hide a smile as I quickly roll her to her belly and grab a pillow to shove under her hips. She looks delectable. I grab one of her asscheeks roughly and squeeze, leaning over to bite the other side.

I'm blinded again, pain searing at my temples and the center of my forehead.

I breathe through it, not letting it stop me from sliding two fingers between her legs to stroke her sweet sex. She's hot and wet, and my canines descend, ready to mark her. My vision clears, but I'm seeing through my wolf-eyes now.

I shove my shorts down enough to free my dick and roll a condom on. "I'm using protection, Pearls."

She slides her legs wider.

I rub the head of my cock over her slit a few times, then nudge in. She arches her back to take me deeper. Gorgeous girl.

Beautiful, hot, incredible little human.

I fill her with my cock and ease back, stroking her insides with my slow thrusts.

I have to breathe deeply and slowly to keep my eyes from going haywire, but I don't care. Being inside Lauren feels like my birthright.

It drives me wild and feels like home at the same time.

I wrap my fist in her hair and tug gently as I pick up the pace. "You didn't let him touch you, did you, beautiful?"

"I gave him a hug at the airport." Lauren tries to look over her shoulder, but my grip on her hair makes it impossible.

I growl—a real wolf growl.

Lauren soaks my dick.

I lean over and growl in her ear. "He never touches you again. Understand?"

I'm harder than stone right now, ready to come, and being close to her shoulder makes my wolf desperate to mark her. "Never," I repeat, picking up speed.

Lauren doesn't answer.

I tug her hair. "Say it."

"Never."

"Good girl." I'm slamming into her now. Both of us are breathless and feverishly hot.

I release her hair to work one nipple, pinching the bud to a stiff peak.

She bites the pillow, crying out in pleasure against the fabric.

"That's right, Pearls. Come for me," I breathe, thrusting faster, losing all sense of place or time.

I slam in deep and fill the condom at the same time her muscles clench and squeeze. She shudders beneath me, sobbing into the pillow with pleasure.

My vision's gone, but there's no pain. I kiss along the back of her neck, rocking slowly to wring out some aftershocks.

"Tomorrow night. After dark. Meet me at the cabin." I don't know if I'm asking or demanding. All I know is that I'm already desperate to see her, and I don't know how I'll make it through the school day without acknowledging she's mine.

I ease out of Lauren and roll her to her back. My vision returns, and I see her lids are heavy, limbs relaxed. She stretches like a cat in the sun. "Maybe," she purrs.

"Meet me," I insist.

She hits me with the beautiful smile again. "'Kay."

I lean over and claim her mouth, kissing her hard. "You're mine now, Lauren Sterling. Nobody else touches you. Nobody else even thinks about you, or I will wolf-smack them down."

Lauren's smile is indulgent, like she's amused by my jealousy, but she shakes her head and points at the window. "Get out, Abe."

Chapter Eighteen

auren
Returning to Wolf Ridge High now that I'm alive again is a new experience. Walking through the hallways, my senses are heightened–or at least no longer dulled. I hear every noise. Notice the natural beauty and spectacular athleticism of most every student I pass—male and female alike.

"Have you noticed how ethnically un-diverse this school is?" I say to Lincoln as we walk to our lockers.

He snorts. "You just now figured that out?"

"I wasn't paying much attention before." I look at him, wondering what he sees. If he's noticed any clues about the differences between the students here and normal human teens.

Lincoln is pretty observant. He's the kind of guy who clocks everyone in the room at a party. He knows their vibe before they ever interact. He always approached our move here as a study in small-town anthropology.

"It's not like Landhower had much diversity," Lincoln

says as he drops his books in his locker and pulls out a notebook and pencil.

"No, but more than here."

"True."

Abe and his friends come strutting down the hallway, talking in loud voices. The other students part to let them sail through.

I'm unprepared for how it feels to have him completely ignore me. He just walks on by with his friends like everything that happened over the weekend didn't happen.

I know he wants it to be a secret that I know about his kind. He feels he can't associate with me. This isn't much different from how he acted last week, after I'd found out he's a wolf.

But last week, I didn't care.

Last week, I was still half-dead. Only just beginning to wake up when I was around Wolf Ridge High's star quarterback.

This week, I feel alive again. And I don't care for being dissed by the school bully who happened to be in my bed last night.

I'd prefer his harassment to this. At least that was attention.

I'm not used to feeling invisible.

I slam my locker and toss my hair as I walk in the opposite direction. When I sit down in my English class, my phone buzzes with a text. I'm instantly certain it will be from Abe.

I sneak a look at it when the teacher isn't looking.

Abe: You look smoking hot today.

My irritation eases. At least he knows he was a dick. He's trying to make up for it.

I sweat him by not answering.

It works. When I see him in the hall after first period, his gaze burns through me. His eyes glint ice blue, and I watch his handsome face tighten.

He's having one of his episodes.

Was it brought on by me again?

I instantly regret my torture of him. Now that I know to look beneath all the alpha-hole swagger, I can see what he's hiding.

He covers it so well, though. When we pass, he throws on a jaunty smirk. "What's up, Pearls?" he jeers, but I can tell his eyes aren't focusing. He probably can't even see me right now.

"Eat me, Abe," I call back breezily.

He laughs, and his friends chortle and scoff. He turns around, walking backward to face me. "Is that an offer, princess?"

I don't turn around. "In your dreams, jock."

Abe's light chuckle sounds genuine.

At lunch, I try to figure out if Rayne is a wolf, too. I meant to ask Abe. I'll add it to the list of questions I have about all things wolf.

She seems to be getting more attention today–kids saying hi to her or waving. I'm sure it has something to do with her being Homecoming Queen although I never got the full story on that. I know she was upset when it happened because she thought her stepbrother orchestrated it, and then she didn't come to school the next day.

Today, it seems epically clear what a non-friend I've been to Rayne, who is literally the only student at Wolf Ridge who has been remotely friendly to me and Lincoln. I was so much in my own muffled bubble, I never cared enough about anybody else.

Abe dogged on me for being stuck-up. I now see that

must be exactly what I seemed like to everyone at this school.

"So...how was Homecoming?" I ask, waggling my brows. "Lincoln said your parents know about you and your stepbrother now?"

Rayne flushes. "It was amazing. I'm really happy."

"So how does it work? Do you just share a bedroom now or what?"

She flushes some more. "Technically, I've been in his bedroom this whole time, and he's been sleeping on the couch. But he's going back to college this week."

"Oh, bummer. Where does he go?"

"Duke."

"Ooh, that's far. I'm sorry."

"No, it's okay. He's going to finish out this year and then see if he can transfer to ASU, where I'm planning to go next year. How about you? Did you break up with your man?"

"Yep. We ended it. It was awkward as hell. But he and Lincoln drove down to ASU after Homecoming and apparently hooked up with college girls, so all good now."

"Oh wow. And you were fine with this?"

Lincoln darts a glance at me. He and I haven't talked about the fact that Abe drove me home that night and what happened afterward. He's giving me privacy.

"Totally fine. It was a relief, actually."

"And how was the rest of your night?" Lincoln asks.

"Uneventful," I say firmly to cut off further inquiry. "Did you hear the wolves after the Homecoming dance?" I ask Rayne. "It sounded like a whole pack of them."

"Oh, really? No, I didn't hear anything."

"You've seen them before, though, right?" I ask, trying to sound casual.

Rayne blinks her big blue eyes and takes a long moment

to swallow her food. "Um, yeah. I've seen wolves a few times."

"How about bears?"

She raises her brows. "No. Why? Did you see one?"

I nod. "Our dad claims there was one on our property. So we've had wolves and bears. I'm starting to think the animals in this town are trying to run us off."

Rayne chokes on her food.

And that's my answer. She's definitely one of them. So she's probably unpopular because she's small and unathletic. Something about the pack order.

"We need to get rid of that shotgun Dad bought," Lincoln mutters darkly.

A chill rushes over my skin. "You're right." It's not just Abe's life that might be at risk with my dad owning a gun. By the way Rayne's eyes round in dismay, I deduce that Lincoln's told her about our dad's attempted suicide.

"How do you safely get rid of a gun?" I muse. "Maybe we just hide it somewhere in the house."

"Yeah," Lincoln agrees. "I'll put it under my bed or something. That way, if that wolf comes back, you and I know where it is."

My stomach knots up at the thought of Lincoln taking a shot at Abe. "We don't even know how to shoot a gun," I argue.

Lincoln shrugs. "I'd figure it out if I had to."

"Well, I don't think you'll have to," I say quickly. "I don't think that wolf is rabid. I think it's friendly. It's probably being fed by humans, so it's not afraid or something."

Rayne nods. "I agree. I wouldn't worry about wolf attacks. I've never heard of anything like that."

"A wolf literally tried to jump through my sister's

window," Lincoln says. "It busted the screen open and everything."

Rayne's gaze flicks to the table where the alpha-holes sit.

Yep. She's one of them, and she knows it was Abe.

I'll have to be extra careful around her. I don't know if I can trust her not to turn me in if she suspects I know their secret.

And there's no way in hell I'm ever letting anyone take me near a vampire again. They'd have to kill me first.

The bell rings, and I stand only to find Abe and his friends right behind me. He ignores me again–or pretends to–but I feel the lightest of touches at my lower back as he passes by, a fleeting acknowledgment that this weekend was real.

School bully Abe is a fake.

When I get to my next class another text comes through.

Abe: Meet me at the cabin tonight. 6:30. I won't disappoint.

My heart revs up like an engine just started. My body heats, remembering all his less-than-disappointing skills. I am definitely going to meet him.

Still, I don't answer.

If he wants to pretend I don't exist, I'm going to make him suffer.

Abe: You told the whole school you want me to eat you. I just want to give you what you need.

Me: I'll think about it.

Abe: I'll be waiting. If you don't come, punishment will be in order.

* * *

After dinner, I tell Lincoln and my dad I'm going to the library, and I drive the Tesla toward the dirt roads that lead toward Abe's cabin.

The trouble is, the roads aren't marked or named, and it's not like I have an address I can plug into the Tesla map system.

I do know the way by foot, though. I end up pulling to the side of the road and parking to hike there. The sun has just set, leaving the mountains glowing a magical pink and purple.

I get a dopamine hit as I walk, knowing what awaits me. For the first time, I actually absorb the beauty my mom saw here—not in an unemotional, flat way, but I feel it in my chest. Like a balloon that expands and makes me feel lighter.

I didn't wear proper footwear for the hike—I'm in a pair of Manolo Blahnik leather flip-flops, but I shouldn't be too far from the cabin or the road that leads to the cabin now.

It's rockier than I remembered, though, and I have to pick my way over the larger stones, avoiding the prickly things. One of the rocks shifts under my feet, and before I even see the danger, a snake curled beneath it strikes my ankle.

I scream and kick, falling on my hands and knees.

The snake slithers back under the rocks.

Oh God. Was it a rattlesnake? Am I in big trouble right now?

I try to climb to my feet, but I only hobble a few steps before I can no longer bear weight on the foot. It swells to twice its size in less than sixty seconds.

My hands shake. My breath is coming in audible sobs. I'm already going into shock. I reach for my phone, but it must have fallen out when I tripped. Darkness is falling fast as I try to crawl back.

Oh fuck.

Please no. Please tell me this isn't happening. I see my phone sticking out of the same crevice the snake disappeared into.

There's no way in hell I'm reaching my hand in there.

And if I thought I wasn't already completely fucked, things get even worse. Because I hear the scrape of rocks behind me.

It's not another snake.

It's worse.

A giant grizzly bear barrels toward me on four legs, its giant maw open in a roar.

* * *

Abe

She didn't come.

I'm not as cocky as I pretend to be, but I *did* think she would come. I *know* she enjoyed our time together this past weekend. She said I made her feel things again.

I *know* she's not hung up on that ex of hers.

So why isn't she here?

I check my phone for the fifteenth time to see if she's answered any of my texts, but she hasn't.

I step out on the porch of the cabin, trying to decide what to do. Should I go to her place? If so, do I go in wolf form to spy or stay in my human form and crawl in her window again?

I'm caught suddenly by my brain glitching, and I stumble back against the cabin, pain searing behind my eyes and through my skull. I gasp and pant, trying to calm my body and bring my human eyes back.

Is Lauren near? I didn't catch her scent. That's not what set me off.

The hairs at the back of my neck stand up. This feels different.

Something's...wrong. Very wrong.

Even though I can't see, I force my legs to move toward my Range Rover. The need to get to Lauren overwhelms me.

Before my vision clears, I hear the crack of underbrush. The sound of something big moving very quickly toward me.

I tense, my body preparing to shift to protect myself. I catch the scent of the bear the moment before my vision clears. It eats up the space between us with a huge bounding gait. I'm about to shift, but I catch sight of something between its powerful jaws.

A woman's sandal.

Lauren's sandal.

Rage spikes, and my wolf is irrationally prepared to fight this bear to the death if he harmed her. But the bear tosses his great head and throws the sandal at my feet, then wheels around.

"Where is she?" I shout as I pick it up. I'm already racing behind him.

He bellows loudly–a spine-tingling sound–but keeps running, so I follow.

My rational brain is starting to follow. He didn't hurt her. He came here to get me. But she is hurt, then. Something's very wrong.

That knowledge makes me run faster than I ever have before in human form. I nearly catch up with the bear.

And then I hear Lauren's screams.

"Help!"

"Lauren!" I shout back, racing even faster. "I'm coming! Where are you?"

"Abe! Please. Over here." She's crying. Definitely scared.

My wolf is frantic. I'm frantic.

"Lauren!" I find her on her ass on some large rocks. Her knees are skinned up, and the foot with the missing sandal is ginormous.

I crouch beside her. "Did you fall? What happened, baby?"

She's crying—sort of hysterical, hyperventilating sobs. "It was a snake!"

"Oh shit." Her swollen flesh is streaked with dark marks up her veins, and I spy the puncture-marks at the ankle. "A rattlesnake?" I scoop her into my arms, turning to look for the bear, but he's disappeared.

"I don't think so. I mean, it didn't rattle."

I start running back toward my vehicle. This is bad. It must be a rattlesnake bite. The dark streaks are the poison traveling toward her heart. Will it kill her? I know they're poisonous to humans. I'm not sure how deadly.

"No, some don't. Humans kill the ones who rattle, so they're evolving not to warn us anymore."

Lauren wraps her arms around my neck. I try not to jostle her too much as I run as fast as I can back to the car. "Don't worry, baby. I'm going to get you to the hospital. Or to my dad. Or whatever it is you need. It's going to be okay."

"After the snake bit me, a bear tried to attack me." Lauren sounds insulted.

"What do you mean attack?"

"Like he came right at me. I screamed and threw rocks until he left."

"I think that bear saved you. He brought your shoe to me, so I'd follow him back."

She quiets, her sobs subsiding, some of the tension in her body draining. "He did?"

"Yeah." I get to the Range Rover and throw open the passenger door then dial my dad as I jog around to the driver's side.

"Dad, I'm with Lauren Sterling, and she just got bit by a rattlesnake."

"Where are you?"

I only hesitate a moment. Lauren's life is at stake. I can deal with explaining what I'm doing with a human later. "At the cabin."

"She needs to get to a hospital, but I have anti-venom at the office. I'll meet you there and ride with you to the hospital."

"Be there in ten." I end the call and look over at Lauren. She's pale, her teal-colored eyes standing out against her skin. "My dad's a doctor. He has anti-venom at the office. We're going to meet him there on the way to the hospital."

She nods. "My phone is still back there. It fell in the crevice where the snake went, so I couldn't call for help."

"Oh, baby. That's so awful. I'm sorry this happened to you."

"It hurts so bad. I think I'm going to puke." She rolls her window down and leans her head out of the window. After a few moments, she asks, "So was the bear a shifter?"

She had texted me over the weekend asking if there was such a thing as a bear shifter, and I told her yes.

"Yeah. An old one. He's not supposed to be on wolf territory, but I've seen him before. In fact, I saw him that day you almost fell off the cliff too. I never told you, but he had your letter. I had to appeal to him to get it back."

"You talked to him?"

"No, he stayed in bear form. I don't know if he's going senile and that's why he's out of his own territory, or what."

I drive faster than is safe down the dirt roads, then three times the speed limit in town to get to my dad's office.

He's waiting out front with his emergency bag. He throws open the passenger door. "Hi, Lauren. I'm Dr. Oakley, Abe's dad. I have an anti-venom I'm going to administer to you before we drive to the hospital, okay?"

"Okay." Lauren's voice is thin and wobbly.

I ditch my plan to pretend I just happened across her. The need to soothe and care for her is far too strong. I reach over and massage her nape while my dad gives her the shot.

If he notices I'm way too intimate with this human, he doesn't let on. He just climbs in the back seat and buckles his seat belt.

I take off for the hospital down in Cave Hills. "Have you called your dad, yet?" my dad asks.

"Her phone is in the snake's hole," I explain.

"Well, you have a phone. He should meet us there. This is serious, son." Now I hear the judgment in my dad's voice.

"Is she going to be okay?" I force myself to ask the question, my heart thudding painfully against my sternum.

"Rattlesnake bites are rarely fatal. About one in six hundred people die from them. How long ago was the strike?"

The word *fatal* bounces around the inside of my skull and makes me press the gas pedal down to the floor.

"Lauren?" my dad prompts when neither of us answer. "How long since you were bitten?"

Lauren is starting to shake. "Um...I'm not sure."

I take off my seatbelt and whip my t-shirt off over my head while still driving seventy miles an hour down the road.

"Abe! What are you doing?" my dad barks.

I drape my t-shirt over Lauren. "She's cold, Dad. She's going into shock or something." I turn the heater on full blast even though it's probably still seventy degrees out. "How long were you there before I got to you?" I ask Lauren.

"I don't know—it felt like forever, but it probably wasn't that long. Fifteen or twenty minutes."

"Okay, so let's say twenty minutes until I got there and another twenty until you gave her the antivenom. Will she be okay?" I try to keep the panic from my voice.

"Yes. She'll be all right. It's serious, though. She'll be in ICU. The venom causes all the organs to shut down."

Intensive care. Fuck!

I hate that this happened on my watch. She was coming to see me. My instincts are to protect her, but I led her into danger. I want to punch my own face.

I reach over to rub her knee, and I find her skin is ice cold. "Lauren?"

The beautiful human is slumped against the car door.

"Dad—*dad*! She passed out cold. What should I do?"

Chapter Nineteen

Lauren

Ugh.

I open my eyes to a ceiling of rectangle fluorescents.

I try to move, but there's an IV hooked up to my arm, and the pain in my foot and ankle is unbearable.

I groan into an oxygen mask.

How long has it been since I got bit? I remember pieces of arriving here, and being moved around and poked and prodded. Has it been one day? Three? Where's my family—Lincoln or my dad. Where's Abe?

"Good. You're awake." I blink as an extremely large doctor steps through the open door. The white coat looks too small for his broad shoulders. Bushy white eyebrows frame his eyes.

I pull down the oxygen mask. "How long have I been here?" I croak.

"It's been thirty hours since you were brought in."

"Is my dad here? Or my brother?"

"It's late. They went home to sleep. How are you feeling?"

"Awful. My whole leg is throbbing."

"Any extreme heat? Tingling? Achy bones? Gnawing hunger?"

"I-I don't know."

He produces a mason jar filled with a brown liquid. "I need you to drink this whole thing down."

I may be groggy, but I'm not stupid. No doctor dishes out medicine in a mason jar.

I attempt to sit up.

"Take it easy, there." He scoops an arm behind me and easily lifts me to sitting.

I gape. "Who are you?"

He looks down at the nametag on his white coat. "I'm Dr. Wesson." He looks back up and thrusts the jar at me with a large gnarled hand. "Now drink this. All at once, so you get the right dosage."

"What is it?"

"Bear brush tea. Unless you want to spend the next week in this ICU, you'll drink that whole jar down right now."

Bear brush tea.

I don't take the jar from him. "*You're* the bear," I accuse triumphantly. I'm glad my fuzzy brain could figure anything out right now. "You led Abe to find me."

This sets him in motion. He caps the jar and tucks it beside me on the hospital bed then backs up toward the door. "Drink the tea, Lauren," –he points a finger at me as he steps through the open doorway– "If you want to get out of here without a limp. That's the only thing that's going to heal you." He starts to go then turns. "I put honey in it, so it won't taste so bad." And then he's gone, pulling off his surgery cap and shrugging out of the doctor's coat as he stalks down the hall.

I stare after him, trying to remember what happened the night I got bit. The bear came bounding toward me. It reached those long arms out for me. Was he trying to pick me up? All I saw was claws and fangs. I thought he was trying to attack me, so I screamed and threw rocks. He must have realized I wasn't going to let him help me, so he went for Abe.

I uncap the mason jar and sniff. It does smell like honey. I bring it to my lips and take a tiny sip. The moment I do, my body is hungry for it.

It's like when you're thirsty, and you take a sip of water but then find yourself gulping down the whole glass. I drain the jar before I even know what I'm doing. As soon as I finish, my brain clears.

The throbbing in my leg eases. I can breathe deeply.

I look around. There's no light coming through the windows. The clock reads one. *In the morning?* I guess so.

I want out of here. Heat and tingles flush my body. I pull the IV out of my arm and throw back the blankets. I suddenly can't stand to be cooped up inside for another minute. If I don't get some fresh air, I'm going to pass out.

I swing my legs off the bed and gingerly put weight on my feet. My ankle throbs, but holds me.

I spot my clothes folded in a corner and hobble over. My phone is sitting on top of the pile, as well. Abe must have gone after it for me.

I hear people talking in the hallway and freeze, but they pass by without looking inside. I hurriedly pull on my clothes and slip my feet into the flip flops. My foot is still swollen, and there are angry dark lines going up my leg, but the heat and tingling has traveled in that direction, almost as if it's flushing away the poison.

I slip out through the door, keeping my head down and walking quickly until I find my way out of the hospital where I gulp in the fresh air.

I keep moving, some urgency to get away from the hospital and the city in general pressing me forward. That's when I spot Abe's Range Rover.

Abe is inside, sleeping against the driver's door like he's been here the entire thirty hours.

I knock on the window, and he jerks awake. "Lauren!" He throws the door open and wraps me in a giant hug. "Fates, what are you doing out of your hospital bed? How are you even walking?"

"Abe, thank God you're here. I'm fine. Sore, but totally fine. Just dying to get home."

Abe cradles my face, peering into it, his brows down. "Yeah." He sounds surprised. "You look good. So much better than you did a few hours ago. Your dad let me come into the room to see you."

I don't know what stops me from telling him about the bear and the tea, but I hold that information back. For some reason, it feels like something just between the old bear shifter and me right now.

"Take me home?"

"Of course." Abe releases me in degrees, like he's reluctant to let go of me. Then he seems to change his mind and scoops me into his arms to walk around to the passenger side of the car.

I laugh. "I can walk okay. I have a bit of a limp, but it's not too bad."

"I don't care," he says gruffly. "I nearly died thinking you were suffering, and there was nothing I could do."

"Are you going to carry me through the halls at school, too?" I ask.

Of course, I already know the answer. He can't. He won't.

I'm the lowly human he can't be associated with. He says it's for my protection, and maybe it is, but I don't like being anyone's dirty little secret. Abe and I are in a no-man's-land. A forbidden relationship with stolen moments.

He sets me on the seat. I see regret in his eyes. "Listen. About us—I told my dad you were out for a hike, and I heard you calling for help, but considering your dad said you were supposed to be at the library, it was obvious I was lying."

"Well, just because he knows we were meeting doesn't mean I know anything about what you are, right?"

Abe stands in the car doorway, his palms lightly stroking up and down my thighs. "That's probably true." His brows are low. "I won't let anything else happen to you, Lauren. I promise."

I believe him. There's no doubt in my mind he cares for me. He may pretend I mean nothing to him in public, but I saw how afraid he was when I got bit by the snake. He would've done anything to save me.

I wrap my fist in his t-shirt and pull him in close, smashing my lips against his. The moment we start kissing, I flush with a feverish heat, tingles igniting all across my skin. My foot gives a painful throb.

I don't care. I'm the opposite of numb right now. I'm full of power, full of life, and falling hard for this wolf-jock who seems to be an integral part of my new identity.

* * *

Abe

"What's going on with you and the human?" My dad hurls the question at me the moment I walk through the door after dropping Lauren at home. I guess he was waiting up for me. He flicks the television off.

I knew this conversation was coming, but I still don't have a good answer.

Shifters can smell lies. No part of me thinks my dad believed my story about happening across Lauren while she was hiking. Especially considering I ditched practice today to go straight to the hospital after school.

This is back to sticking close to the truth, even though my dad will hate it.

"I don't know." I shrug, trying to look casual. Like my entire life doesn't revolve around that beautiful human. "We hooked up at Homecoming. I was going to hook up with her again yesterday, but she got bit by the snake on her way to meet me. I had to make sure she was all right." I spin my keyring around my index finger like it's no big deal. Like my heart didn't almost stop beating when I found her there in agony.

My dad frowns. He won't detect any lie because it's all true.

"Coach Jamison called to say you missed practice. You don't miss practice without getting his prior approval. You know that."

Yeah, but I wasn't thinking rationally.

"I felt an episode coming on, and I thought it would be better to stay away from the team. Plus, I had to bring Lauren her phone."

Also not a lie. The stress and worry over Lauren is killing me. Today, the lack of her scent at school brought on a headache that didn't leave until she got into my vehicle tonight.

My dad gets up off the couch and pulls a penlight out of his pocket, shining it in my eyes. I stand stiffly for the examination.

"You look fine now," my dad observes, turning the light off and putting it back in his pocket. "There are scouts from three different schools coming to your game Thursday night, and you decide it's better to skip practice? Are you *trying* to ruin your future?"

Lauren is my future, my wolf snarls.

"I don't even know if I can get through college at this rate, Dad," I explode.

He jerks back, like I punched him, his mouth opening in shock.

"I can't read papers that get handed out, I can't focus on the words on the board. It's all fine and dandy if I get a football scholarship to ASU, but I don't know how I'll pass my classes."

My mom emerges from their bedroom at the sound of my raised voice. "Honey, I didn't know it was getting that bad."

"Neither did I," my dad says.

The scent of my mom's distress reaches both of us, and my dad's instinct to soothe her apparently overrides his need to grill me. He reaches for my mom and pulls her against his side, wrapping one arm protectively around her waist.

"We can run more tests," my dad says. "There has to be a way to identify your triggers and reduce their incidences."

"I don't want to be your lab rat anymore!"

"Abe," my mom warns.

"What is your solution, son?" My dad's tone is sharp. "You can't function at school, but you don't want to identify your triggers. How am I supposed to help you?"

"You're supposed to lay off when I'm doing the best I can! I don't need or want you to solve my problems for me. This is *my* life. Let me figure it out for myself!" I leave without being dismissed, stomping down the hall to my room.

* * *

After a grueling practice in which Coach Jamison makes me do push-ups in between every play as penance for missing yesterday, I shower and drive up to Moongaze Hill.

Lauren didn't come to school today, but I've been texting with her, and she says she feels good and only stayed home because her dad was freaked out that she'd left the hospital without being discharged.

She said I could pick her up to go for a drive after practice.

I know it's reckless. Being seen with her would completely fuck my reputation, but I can't seem to help myself. I need her scent up in my nostrils. Crave touching her luscious body. I need to see with my two eyes that she's really okay.

I park in front of her house and take the steps up to the door. Halfway there, I suddenly get nervous. I've lived in Wolf Ridge my whole life. My parents are pack royalty, my brother was class president and a football star, and I'm the team captain of Wolf Ridge High. There's nowhere in this town I go where people don't already know and respect me. But here I am knocking on the door of a human. I might have to look and sound respectable if I meet her dad.

As it turns out, it's Lincoln who answers the door.

His eyes narrow as he surveys me, but he steps back from the door to let me in. I saw him at the hospital Monday night after my dad and I brought Lauren in, but other than me repeating my story about finding Lauren bitten on a trail, we didn't have much to say to each other.

"Lauren!" he calls out, keeping a suspicious gaze on me.

"Hey," I say.

"What exactly are you doing with my sister, Oakley?"

I shrug. Jeez. First my dad, now Lincoln. "Just hanging out."

"Yeah? You've been a dick to her since school started, and suddenly, you want to hang out? I don't get it."

A sick feeling rolls through me. I didn't think my assholery had bothered Lauren. She seemed completely impervious to it, but her twin bringing it up makes me fear I hurt her.

Lauren appears behind Lincoln. She's hardly limping at all—just walking a little gingerly, and far from appearing sickly, her skin, her face, her countenance appear positively luminescent. "Eh, he's still a dick, but I can handle him." She sails right by her brother and me, somehow managing to strut out the door with a hurt ankle.

I can't stop the slow grin from spreading across my face. "That she can," I mutter, spinning my keys around my finger as I follow her out, my eyes trained on her juicy ass, which looks amazing in a pair of black shorts that mold to her curves.

I hear Lincoln make a disapproving sound as he shuts the door, but I don't care. I'm back in the same airspace with Lauren—exactly where my wolf was dying to be.

I run to get to the passenger door first, opening it like a gentleman then picking her up by the waist to lift her in.

"Show off," she says.

Fates she feels so receptive right now. There's something different about her. If possible, she seems even hotter than before. Her tits swell beneath a tight crop top. Her shapely legs look more tan than before, and the flat plane of her belly looks entirely too kissable.

I shut the door and walk around to my side, climbing in. "How can I thrill you?" I ask as I start the car.

Lauren's laugh is throaty. Sexy as fuck. "What are my options?"

"Cliff diving? A roller coaster? Drag racing? No—scratch that—there's no way I'm putting you in real danger again."

Her smile is soft and inviting. Utterly intoxicating. "I was thinking something more along the lines of a cabin in the woods. Minus the rattlesnake I ran into on the way last time."

The cabin. My wolf fist pumps the air. I was right about her energy being receptive. I don't know what changed—whether it was my rescuing her when she was scared or proving I cared by hanging around the hospital afterward—but there's an energy she's sending me now that is undeniable.

My temples throb with a muscle spasm behind my eyes. I blink rapidly and hold my breath to keep from inhaling her scent until it passes.

"Cabin in the woods, it is." I take off, driving the short distance to the road that leads out to the cabin.

"Ah, so *here's* where the road is," Lauren says. "I couldn't find it, so I parked and tried to walk there."

I groan. "I wish you had called me, Pearls."

She groans ruefully. "So do I."

I park at the cabin and turn off the engine. "Tell me I get to tie you up again."

She throws open her door. "Catch me if you can!" She

leaps from the Rover and bolts toward the woods, the slight hobble in her run making her look adorable.

My dick, already long in my pants just from being near her, gets rock hard. I race after her, catching her before she gets into the woods and spinning her around. I swing her up over my shoulder to run to the cabin, where I open the front door and step through.

Lauren bites my back, squeezes my ass. She's more feral than a she-wolf tonight.

It's so hot.

I set her gently down on the sofa. Despite our play, I'm still on edge thinking about her near-death experience with the rattlesnake. If I cause her even one bit of additional pain tonight, I'd kick my own balls.

The moment I set her down, she fists my shirt and pulls me down beside her on the couch with more strength than I gave her credit for. I guess human females aren't entirely weak.

She climbs over my lap, tearing my t-shirt off over my head.

"Oh, okay," I laugh. "So that's how we're playing this."

She bites my shoulder, rocking her hips over my aching dick.

"You wanna tie me up this time, pearls?"

She unbuttons my shorts.

"Ahhuh" I groan when she pulls my erection out with a firm grip.

"I just wanna be on top tonight." She slides off the sofa and onto her knees. When she takes my cock between those pouty lips, sucking on the tip, I let out another groan. At this rate, I'm not going to last more than a minute.

"I guess that snakebite was the best near death experience yet. You're more than alive right now, baby. You're on fire."

She takes more of my cock into her mouth, and I shudder with pleasure. "I do feel alive," she says, popping off and stroking her fist up and down my already enormous erection.

She takes my cock back in her mouth, bobbing her head up and down over it, driving me mad. She comes off and unbuttons her shorts, rising to her feet. "I feel so alive. And I'm really turned on right now."

I almost orgasm right there. There is nothing hotter than beautiful, glorious Lauren Sterling turned on. The scent of her arousal drugs me. I reach out to help her slide her shorts and panties down as she kicks off her fancy flip-flops.

"Come here, baby." I take her hands and pull her toward me. She starts to straddle my waist, but I lift her hands higher until she's standing on my thighs, and then I lift one knee and drape it over my shoulder, so I can get my mouth between her legs.

"Oh, Abe." She grabs the back of my head and angles her pussy, so I can access more of it. I part that sweet fruit with my tongue, swirling around her clit. She tastes delicious. Different than before. Sweeter. More potent. Absolutely perfect.

The need to mark her comes on so fast, I almost bury my lengthened canines in her thigh. I jerk back, now blinded by my body's glitch.

To cover, I pick her up by the waist and lie her on her back on the sofa.

"Abe." She pulls me down over her, but then arrests my descent, with a hand pressed to my chest. "Oh. You're having an episode, aren't you?"

"Yeah." It's a relief to be able to admit it to her. To not

have to hide it like I do with everyone else in my life, including my parents.

"What do you need?"

I shake my head, trying to shake off the pain. "No, I'm good." It's partially true. I can see out of the periphery of my vision.

Lauren pushes me away. "Then let me do the work." We trade places, and she straddles my waist, gripping my dick to rub it through her slick juices.

"Oh, fates." Pain seizes my temples but only because it's so good. Only because my wolf is in a frenzy because I haven't marked her yet. "Lauren, you drive me crazy." I grip her hips, lifting her up to line up her entrance with the head of my cock. I impale her.

She settles down on my hips with the female version of a growl, rocking forward and back to get in deeper.

So hot. This girl is blowing my mind right now.

I thrust up into her, but she presses down on my shoulders. "I'm driving, baller."

I force myself to go still for her, and she rides me, finding her own rhythm. She moves to a position that must satisfy her because she stays there, working harder, moving with more intensity. My vision clears enough to see her face scrunching in the cutest look of concentration.

The moment she comes, I go fully blind. I shoot my wad, my hips bucking as I grip her waist and hold her down over me.

Her internal muscles squeeze around my dick, milking it.

I'm not sure if I passed out again or was just swept away with the orgasm, but the next thing I know, Lauren's hands are covering my eyes.

I hold her wrists to keep her fingers in place. I find the

light touch soothing, like she can smooth away the buzzy and spasticity beneath my lids. She doesn't ask if I'm all right. She's not telling me to do something like breathe or relax. She's just here with me, knowing exactly what's going on and accepting it.

After a few moments, the pain subsides. I gently pull her fingertips away and open my eyes. Thank fuck–I can see her. She's surrounded with a halo of luminescence, like the moon goddess herself.

She smiles slowly when she realizes I can see again. "You're back," she says softly.

"Yeah."

I pull her down to my chest, the need to mark her passing, replaced by a far more tender urge to simply hold her.

"It's weird," I say against her hair. "I've lived in Wolf Ridge my whole life. I grew up with my best friends J. J., Markley, Asher and Sebs. And you're this stranger here– this human I've known for less than two months. But for some reason, it feels like you might know me better than anyone."

Lauren pushes herself back to look at my face. She runs her fingertips lightly around the shells of my ears, sending pops of pleasure through my system.

"Same," she whispers.

Chapter Twenty

*L*auren

I walk through the halls at Wolf Ridge with an odd sense of power coursing through me.

I still haven't told a soul about drinking that bear brush tea, but I am quite certain it's the reason I feel so incredible. I woke up this morning with more energy than I've ever felt. My ankle still shows the black streaks of poison going up my leg, and it's still slightly swollen, but it doesn't hurt at all.

My reflection in the mirror showed a young woman vibrating with well-being and life. I'm luminous. A far cry from the barely-living numb girl incapable of grieving I was just a few weeks ago.

Where I didn't care about making friends at Wolf Ridge High before, now I look around with an air of benevolent superiority. I suddenly see I can have any friend I want with minimal effort. I realize that's always been true, but I hadn't put any effort into it before.

I didn't believe anyone here was worth my energy, but it was because I wasn't giving *myself* any energy. I'd blocked off the flow of my own life force.

When I walk into Chemistry, Abe's gaze snaps to me, then he quickly looks away. He keeps his head down during class, taking notes–possibly for the first time, ever.

Last night, I felt so connected with him, but today he's back to pretending I'm nothing. The wound wouldn't have even hit before. But that was when I didn't care. When I felt nothing.

Now, it dents me. My magnificent mood caves in on itself.

Abe texts me toward the end of class. **You look good enough to eat.**

I don't reply.

Another text comes through: **I have a game tonight, but I want to see you.**

I ignore it. I'm tired of being his dirty little secret. I don't like feeling like I'm not good enough because I'm not a wolf.

Somehow, I sense Abe's agitation from my non-reply. I don't look his way, but when I get up to leave at the end of class, I feel his gaze burning into my back.

"What's up, Ice Princess?" one of his cronies–Asher, I think–calls out as he passes me by. He chortles and holds out a fist for Abe to bump, which means he must be right behind me.

I stop and give him my full attention. "What's up with you, loser?" I call in a cheery voice.

Asher stops, too.

Abe bumps into me from behind. His hand finds my hip. I knock it away.

We're blocking all the traffic in the crowded hallway now.

"Ooh, too good for all of us, aren't you, rich girl?"

"Lay off," Abe growls.

Asher looks over in surprise.

I sense Abe take a step back, away from me. I turn to look and see his nostrils are flaring, and his eyes have turned ice-blue. He looks off-balance. I'm not sure if he can see anything right now. He's having one of his episodes.

"Dude... you're, um–" Asher taps his temple.

Abe crashes to the floor in a dead heap. His head slams against the hard linoleum with a sickening crack.

"Oh shit." I drop to my knees beside him.

Abe's body convulses. I don't know if it was his fronting that made me believe he really could handle what was going on with him before, but I realize that was all just bluster. Abe has a serious medical problem he's been covering up for fear of appearing weak. Terror strikes through my heart now.

"He's having a seizure!" I call out. "Get a teacher." I cradle his head to keep it from banging against the ground. Abe's legs jerk, his body flops.

Oh, God.

Bodies crowd around us, kids pressing in to see, everyone staring.

"Get back," I wave an arm. My stomach is in my throat. "Somebody get help!"

Tears smart my eyes.

Abe sucks in a hard breath with a huge whoosh, then sits up, gasping. He blinks, his eyes changing back to slate grey. He looks around at everyone staring at him. "Fuck." In a flash, he's on his feet, and I'm still kneeling on the ground.

"Dude," Asher says, eyes wide. "What just happened to you?"

"Abe, you have to stop pretending you're okay, when you're not." I climb to my feet. "You need to get help–this is dangerous. What if that happened while you were driving or something?"

Abe scrubs a hand across his face, taking in the throng of people around us. I should have expected it, but it hits me like a slap when his face contorts into an all-too-familiar expression of scorn. "Don't pretend you know me, Princess." He makes a shooing motion. "Go back to your mansion. You have no idea what's really going on."

What's really going on?

Is that his way of pretending I don't know he's a wolf?

You know what? I don't care. Abe could find a million other ways to protect me. He's just being a dick, as he has always been.

Why I thought I could actually care about someone as flawed as him is beyond me.

"Yeah, keep covering up with bullshit. That's what you're good at."

Abe is already walking away from me, redirecting the crowd away from the scene he was so desperate to avoid. I don't even get the dignity of him waiting for my comeback.

I watch his retreating back–those broad shoulders that look like they belong on a man, not a high school student. My continued attraction to him hits me as pain.

"You're so afraid everyone will think you're weak, Abe," I say to his back.

He doesn't turn but others stop to listen to me. They want to know what I dare say to their king.

"Well, you *are* weak. You're so afraid of showing who you really are to the people around you, and it makes you the biggest coward in this school."

He rounds the bend without ever looking back.

I blink rapidly, fighting the hot tears threatening behind my eyes.

Rayne appears at my elbow, her expression wide and

concerned. "You okay?" she murmurs, taking my arm and pulling me in the opposite direction of Abe.

"No." I fight down the swell of emotion choking me. "But I will be." I square my shoulders and hold my head up high as I march out the school.

I don't need Abe Oakley.

I have me now.

He and all his alpha-hole friends can go screw themselves.

I'm officially done.

* * *

Abe

I shake the crowd by heading into the locker room, even though we don't have practice today because of the game tonight.

I just fucked up. Big time.

It takes me a few minutes to realize the reason my heart is pounding, and I'm cold with dread. It's not because the whole school just saw me have some kind of seizure. It's not because a human just called me a coward in front of everyone.

It's because I hurt Lauren.

The moment I pull my head out of my ass, I run out the doors toward the parking lot. "Lauren!" I spot her getting into the passenger side of the Tesla.

She tosses her copper hair and slams the door shut.

I drop my backpack and run toward the car. I need to fix this before it's too late.

The bile in my throat tells me that ship has sailed, though.

The Tesla is exiting the parking lot. I sprint toward it,

reaching just as they get to the gate. "Lauren!" I thump the back of the car with my hand, like tagging it will somehow make them stop.

Lincoln and Lauren both completely ignore me. Lincoln hits the accelerator, and the Tesla shoots out of the gates, zipping into traffic and leaving me standing on the corner, panting.

Fuck.

I pull my phone out of my pocket, but I can't text because I can't see a damn thing. Pain stabs through my head. The sunlight hurts my eyes.

My wolf is howling inside me. Howling at me for letting her get away. For damaging what we had.

I am the biggest asshole on campus.

It's honestly not something I was ever proud of. I considered it an act, something separate from my real self, but today it feels true.

"Dude, what happened back there?" Asher appears at my elbow.

I double over in pain. I can't have another seizure. I need to get to Lauren and fix this.

"Fuck. Should I call your dad?"

"No," I pant, straightening again. Even with my lids closed, the harsh Arizona sun sears my sensitive eyeballs. "Can you drive?"

"Yeah. Are you sure?"

For once in my life, I resist the urge to lash out at him to deflect from my weakness. Lauren was right. It's not strength–it's cowardice.

"I can't see," I admit. "My wolf eyes are glitched." I crack my lids, but my eyes are in spasm, and I can't see anything.

"Damn. I can tell. Let's go. Just stick right beside me." Asher's smart enough to know I wouldn't want anyone else to see, even though it's probably way too late for that. "What about tonight's game? There are scouts coming from three different schools."

Heaviness descends over me. "I don't know. I'm probably fucked."

It doesn't matter. The only thing I care about is Lauren.

I find my way in the darkness, using my shifter hearing and sense of smell to stick right beside Asher. He leads me to my Range Rover.

Asher doesn't have his own car–his parents were low status in the pack even before his dad got kicked out–but he has a license.

I hand him my keys and climb in through the passenger door.

"Do you want me to bring you home?"

"No. Take me to Moongaze Hill."

Searing pain grips my temples. Nausea hits at the same time. I slumped low in the seat, trying to recover.

"Dude, I think I should take you home. You don't look so good."

"I'm fine—just drive, asshole."

Asher starts the Rover up and peels out. As we drive, I count measured breaths trying to steady my nervous system. My vision starts to return—first the peripheral and then, finally, my full sight. I slump back against the seat in relief. The roiling in my stomach calms.

I don't know what I'm going to say to Lauren. Words won't be adequate. I'm going to have to make it up to her in some other way. Maybe that's what I'll tell her. I'm going to prove to the whole school that she's mine.

My wolf likes that idea. But there's a nagging sense of unease that tells me something is not right with my plan. Or maybe it's just that it won't work.

Asher turns my car up the road that winds up Moongaze Hill, and my right eye starts twitching. As we drive, the twitching grows. Pain starts in the nerves behind my eyes, traveling back to the base of my skull and down my spine.

I'm panting, hard enough for Asher to notice.

"Abe?"

I squirm in my seat, thrashing my legs. I'm trying to get a grip on this complete and utter fail on the part of my body.

It only gets worse, though. I fight the sensation of being out of control, of my body, taking over and leaving me behind. I roll down the window, even though it's hotter outside. I hang my head out the door sucking in deep breaths.

I can do this. I can make it. We're almost to the Sterling mansion. I just need to get there and talk to Lauren. I just need to fix this.

My body starts to convulse. I can feel my eyes rolling back in my head, but there's nothing I can do to stop.

I lose complete control, my brain, fully detached from the body I'm in. I'm unable to speak.

Fate has royally fucked me this time. I can't help but think that this is my punishment for being cruel to the only female I've ever loved.

* * *

Lauren

"What happened?" Lincoln waits until we're home to ask.

A week ago, I would've shrugged and deflected the intrusion. But everything feels different. I've been awakened. I'm alive. I may not have a mom, but I do have a dad and a brother who both love me.

"You want to take a walk?" I ask.

"Sure." He looks down at my still-swollen ankle. "Is your foot okay?"

"It's fine." It is. It looks even better than it did this morning, even after me walking on it all day. That bear brush tea is truly miraculous.

I change into sneakers and take Lincoln out on the walk to the cliff. You would think I'd be scared to be on the same path that resulted in a snake bite last time, but I'm not. I feel invincible today.

When we get to the cliff, I say, "I came here on the anniversary of Mom's death to read her letter."

Lincoln walks to the edge of the cliff with me and stares down at the desert scrabble below.

"I reread the letter she wrote me that day, too."

I steal a glance at Lincoln. I don't see pain on his face. He's always seemed so grounded about our mom's death. It's weird how we could be twins going through the same thing with such different ways of dealing with it.

"Abe saw me here and thought I was going to jump off the cliff or something. He startled me, and then I did almost fall, but he grabbed me in time."

Lincoln says nothing. He's always been an excellent listener.

"The letter went over the edge, but he went down and found it for me. And then we hung out at his family's cabin, which is a little bit that way."

I leave out the part about him being a wolf, obviously. Not because I promised Abe. I figure he lost my loyalty to his secret when he acted like a dick. But I don't want Lincoln to be in danger of getting his mind wiped by a vampire.

"So you two bonded then," he observes.

"Yeah, I guess. I ended up telling him about Mom and actually cried for the first time since before she died."

Lincoln nods. "That's good."

"Yeah."

"And then we hooked up at homecoming, as you probably guessed, and we met at his cabin a couple of times. But it turns out, the reason he's such an asshole is because he has a medical condition that he's been trying to hide from everyone because he doesn't wanna look weak."

Lincoln swings his head to look at me with surprise. "Wow."

"I know. So today, he was having a seizure in the hall, and when I tried to help, he shit on me. I guess he was ashamed."

"What an asshole. What an absolute child."

"I know. I'm totally done with him."

Except when I say it, it doesn't feel true.

I don't feel like I'm done with Abe Oakley. And retelling his story actually gives me a little more compassion for his plight. Not that the way he treated me is okay.

I realize that I am afraid I won't be able to cry over Abe, just like I couldn't cry over my mom. But it's not because I'm broken. I'm not. I'm numb and locked in a cell of my own making. It's not because I've gone flat again. Because I feel strong. And I have this niggling sense that Abe belongs to me.

That's why I trigger the episodes in Abe. The two of us are inexorably linked. Our fates are locked together. We're meant for each other somehow. Just like I was meant to get bitten by that snake, and I was meant to drink the tea the old bear brought me.

I'm not sure what makes all of this so clear in my mind, but it is. I seem to have some new broader connection with the world around me. Just like I felt more connected to the kids at school. I feel more connected to the nature around us right now. To this land that my mom found so majestic. And my connection to Abe is one thousand times stronger than my connection to anything else.

"You seem good, actually," Lincoln says. "Better than you have since Mom got sick."

I smile. "I know. I feel more like myself than I ever have. And I do have Abe to thank for that because it felt like he sort of woke me up from the numbness and the fog I was living in."

Lincoln turns to me and holds out his arms. "Come here. Want a hug?"

"Yep." I step into the circle of his arms.

"We are going to be okay," Lincoln says. "All of us. You, me, and Dad. It's been a rough year, but we're on the other side now."

I hear the movement of a rock several yards away, and my foolish heart leaps up, thinking it's going to be Abe. It's not. It's the giant grizzly bear with gray fur around the snout, chest, and wrist cuffs.

Lincoln stiffens. I put my hand on his forearm and ease out of the hug. "It's okay," I tell him. "I know this bear."

I lift an arm and wave. "Hey, bear."

The bear rises on two legs and makes a warbling sound.

Lincoln takes a step back, pulling me behind him protectively. The bear stays upright, sniffing the air as he eyes us.

Then he lumbers away, lifting a great paw into the air as he turns.

"Did that bear seriously just wave at us?" Lincoln is in awe.

I laugh softly. "Yeah, he did."

"Mom would've loved that."

"Yeah. I feel like... maybe Mom sent him. Maybe it's her way of watching over us."

My vision gets blurry, but they are happy tears. Despite my epic breakup with a guy I wasn't even supposed to be dating, this day feels significant. Magical in a way.

Because I know what Lincoln said is true. We are all going to be OK. Me. Lincoln. My dad. And Abe. He is part of the equation now. He belongs to me just like I belong to him.

But I can't make him come around. If he wants me back, he will have to fight for us.

And I will fight too.

* * *

Abe

I wake in my dad's clinic.

"Fuck." I sit up fast, making my vision recede into blackness again.

"Easy." My dad pushes me back to prone.

I sense, rather than see, his light moving across my eyes.

"What happened?"

"You tell me, son. Asher said you had a seizure at school and then another one in your car while he was driving."

"Fuck."

"Watch your language."

I sit up again, this time swinging my legs off the cot.

"Whoa. Where are you going? Can you even see right now?"

"What time is it? How long was I out?"

"About ninety minutes. I gave you a short-term sedative to try to relax your nervous system."

I rub my eyes, light bleeding back into my visual field.

"I didn't want it to interfere with the game tonight."

The game tonight. Fuck.

"What time is it?" I stand, blinking. I still feel nauseous. I need to get to Lauren.

"Five o'clock."

Five o'clock. That's the time we're supposed to be in the locker room for the game. But I haven't spoken to Lauren yet. Haven't fixed my mess–if it's even fixable.

"I called Coach to tell him you'll be a few minutes late, but you're coming. He heard about the seizure at school. The whole town has by now." My dad's judgment hits me like a punch to the gut, but I don't flinch.

I walk toward the door.

"Hold up." My dad uses Alpha Command, so my body freezes of its own accord. "I'll drive you there. I don't want you behind a wheel yet."

I growl my dissatisfaction. How will I get to Lauren without my car?

"You could pass out behind the wheel and hit a human." My dad says. "Give me the keys."

Gah. This day couldn't get worse. I hand over the keys, and we walk out to the Rover.

But then it does get worse because as soon as my dad gets behind the wheel, he says, "What happened to the money in my safe?"

My stomach knots. My eye starts to twitch. I flip it back on him in my usual deflective mode. "Really? You're going to grill me right before the game you care so much about?"

"What happened to the money?" My dad's using a form of Alpha Command. The blast of it sears through my skull.

The danger to Lauren makes my wolf snap and snarl. My vision goes dark in the center. The light through the windshield hurts my head.

Stick close to the truth. It's the only solution.

"Lauren saw me shift." I shade my eyes, trying not to show how much pain I'm in. "I called Austin, and he told me about the safe and gave me the contact info for a vampire. I took her there and took care of it."

Close to true. I took care of shooting Thomas when he tried to drain Lauren instead of mind-wiping her.

"Which vampire?"

"His name was Thomas." A shudder runs through me at the memory of Thomas sucking Lauren's blood.

"Thomas. He's not trusted by our kind. That was dangerous, Abe. Taking matters into your own hands is not how things get handled in this pack."

"I know, Dad. I do. But I'd been told to stay away from Lauren. I figured it was better to take care of it myself. And I did."

"You did?" Do I hear doubt in my dad's voice?

"I did." I'm trying to say it firmly, but it comes out as alpha command, and it pushes my dad's body back in the seat.

Whoops.

My dad frowns as he pulls up in front of the school. I throw open the door and hop out. My nose is starting to bleed, my head is killing me, and I can barely see.

I shut the door without waiting for my dad's game advice. I frankly could care less about this game.

I am nothing without Lauren. That's already epically clear.

I've been denying what I knew from day one–she's my mate. The episodes with my vision are worse because my wolf is desperate to mark her.

My only hope is that Lauren will come to the game tonight, and I can somehow make things right.

* * *

Lauren

Lincoln decided to go to the game with Rayne. Her stepbrother left to go back and play for Duke this week, and I guess she wanted company.

After much internal debate, I decide to go with him. The small, wounded part of me hopes my scent will cause Abe another episode while he's out on the field. But no. I don't really want that. I do want him to feel my presence though. I do want him to realize what he's lost. I don't think that's my pride or ego talking. This new, stronger self doesn't believe things should be over. New me believes that we mean something to each other.

Lincoln and I get out of the car and walk toward the stadium. As we approach security to have our bags checked and show our season passes, a sheriff's deputy asks if he can have a word with me.

Lincoln stares at me as the officer pulls me to the side. I expect him to search my bag or something. Like at the airport when you get randomly flagged for a full search. But instead, he signals to another officer, who walks over with a man who seems vaguely familiar.

"Hi, Miss Sterling. I'm Sheriff Gleason. We have some questions for you. Can you come with me, please?"

Lincoln walks over. "What is this about?"

The sheriff turns on him. "It's an open investigation. Your sister is not in trouble, we just need to take her down to the station and ask her a few questions. We will have her back before the end of the game."

My eyes round. What the hell?

Then a shock of fear goes through me. "Is this about Abe?" I realize why the man who is not in a uniform looks familiar. He has slate gray eyes and a square jaw like Abe. "Is he okay?"

The sheriff gently takes my elbow and starts walking me away from the stadium. "We hope so. But we need your help."

I wave Lincoln away. "It's okay. I'll be back."

He frowns after me but doesn't follow.

The sheriff leads me to a patrol car and puts me in the back seat. Abe's dad–at least I'm assuming he's Abe's dad–gets in the passenger side.

"Did something happen to Abe? Did he have another episode?"

That brings his dad's head around. "What do you know about his episodes?"

This is the guy who made Abe hide his affliction instead of helping him. He made him ashamed of it. He created incredible stress that probably only added to the occurrence of his episodes.

I lift my chin and meet his gaze. "I know everything."

Wrong thing to say.

Abe's dad and the sheriff share a look, and I suddenly realize what's happening here. A chill washes over me. I reach for the door handle, even though the car is moving. It's locked.

Oh crap. They found out that I know about wolves. Did Abe tell them?

He wouldn't do that to me, would he? Send me back to the vampire to have my mind wiped?

Then again, we're broken up. Maybe this is how he cleans up his mess.

I try the door handle again, frantically this time. "I want out. I'm not going anywhere with you. Let me go!"

The men in the front share another look. "I can give her a sedative," Abe's dad murmurs to the sheriff.

"It's all right. We're almost there," he answers in an equally low voice. Then he raises the volume when he speaks to me. "It's okay, Lauren. No one is going to hurt you. We just need to ask you some questions down at the station."

I force myself to calm down, pretending to play along as I slowly reach my hand into my purse. I need to text Lincoln.

The car stops. I'm not sure whether to be surprised that they actually took me to the station or not. I whip out my phone, fingers shaking as I try to fire a text message off to Lincoln

The back door flies open, and the sheriff snatches the phone from my hand.

"Give it back!" I lunge for the phone, but the sheriff spins me around and pushes my front against the car, snapping a pair of handcuffs around my wrists.

"This is for your own protection, Lauren. Now, come with me."

I attempt to sit down on the ground. I've heard about protestors making their bodies heavy. It has no effect. These men are shifters. They each lift one of my arms and carry me between the two of them like I'm a toddler swinging between her two parents.

Someone holds open the door for us–a man in a suit. A human?

"Excuse me." I turn to look at him, and the moment he catches my gaze, my entire body goes limp.

Too late.

The vampire is here.

This is the last moment I will know about werewolves or bear shifters...or Abe.

The two men drag my limp body inside. Tears smart my eyes.

Not knowing Abe, not remembering what we had together is a worse fate than the numbness that engulfed me when I moved to Wolf Ridge.

Abe brought me back to life. He made me feel beautiful and strong. He showed me a world I want to inhabit.

And now he's about to be taken from me.

* * *

Abe

I play my ass off in the first quarter of the game, despite a bloody nose, raging headache, and a twitch in one eye.

What keeps me going is the belief that Lauren might be here somewhere. I thought I caught her scent in the breeze although I can't spot her anywhere in the stands. I see Lincoln, though. He stands when he sees me looking and walks down the stairs toward the railing.

Relief sweeps through me. He has a message for me. Some word about Lauren. I jog over to the railing to meet him.

There's an aggressive edge to him that I haven't felt before. This kid is slender, he probably weighs half what I do, so I have to give him credit for the challenge.

"Do you want to tell me why the sheriff and your dad just took my sister to the station for questioning?"

Shock ripples through me. I sense the color drain from my face, and I'm running before I remember that I didn't answer Lincoln.

I rip off my helmet and throw it onto the grass.

"Oakley!" I hear Coach Jamison yell after me as I race out of the stadium. "Get back here right now!" He uses alpha command, but it has no effect on me.

My wolf is in charge, and he's ready to kill.

When I'm out in the parking lot, I remember I don't have a car. My dad dropped me off. That was probably intentional. I start running as fast as I can in human form.

Lincoln and Lauren's Tesla pulls up beside me.

"Get in," Lincoln says through the open window.

I open the door after figuring out the weird handle and throw my body inside, my shoulder pads making it awkward.

Lincoln takes off immediately, and damn, can his car go fast. We are zero to ninety in probably three seconds.

"What happened?" he demands.

I shake my head. "It's a misunderstanding. I'm going to straighten it out right now."

"A misunderstanding." Lincoln's voice has a deadly ring to it. Again, props to the guy for not being afraid of me.

"I'm going to fix it. I fucked up with Lauren today, but I'm going to fix that too." I turn to look at Lincoln, whose normally laid-back expression is grim. "I really care about your sister. I didn't mean to blow it with her. I had my head shoved up my ass so far I couldn't see for a minute."

Lincoln nods. He swerves at the turn and whips into the drive for the sheriff's office.

I open the door. "Wait for me. Don't come in. That will make things worse. I'll be out with Lauren in ten minutes or less."

"You want to tell me what the fuck is going on?" Lincoln demands.

I'm already out of the car. "Nope." I slam the door shut and run inside.

The sheriff's office is small. I ignore Betty Branson at the front desk and follow my shifter hearing to an interrogation room in the back.

"Hold up!" I hear her get up from behind the desk. "You can't go back there, Abe."

I ignore her and try the door. It's locked. I don't wait or knock, I tear at the knob with one foot braced against the concrete wall. The metal door bows, then gives way, and I rip it right off its hinges.

Betty shrieks.

I throw the door behind me. Inside, Lauren's slumped over a table like she's been beaten, her hands handcuffed behind her back.

"Get away from her!" I shove the sheriff's deputy into a wall.

Huge mistake. Lauren's head jerks up at the sound of my voice. The undead asshole standing in front of her leans down to look in her eyes.

"No!" I shout as I slam his head down into the table, busting his nose. And then everything happens at once.

My dad and the sheriff pull me back. The vampire moves lightning fast. One second he's face down on the table, the next he's right in my face, fangs descended, eyes darkened with blood lust.

"Easy, easy, easy. Take a breath." The sheriff uses a soothing voice as he and my dad pull me backward, away from the vampire.

He's not the same one I brought Lauren to before–it's some leech I haven't seen before.

My vision is twitching, my head about to explode from pressure and pain. *"Let go of my mate, or I will destroy everyone in this room."* My voice isn't my own. There's a wolf-growl to it, like I've already half-shifted.

"*Mate.*" Surprise tinges my dad's voice.

"Let her go *now*." I'm done warning them. I headbutt my dad at the same time I kick the sheriff in the gut, twisting out of both of their grasps.

Lauren's on her feet, staring at me in shock. I snatch her against my chest, reaching around to grasp the metal cuffs behind her. With one snap, I break them apart.

"Hold up, Abe." The sheriff still has that calming tone like I'm a feral beast they're trying to contain.

Which I guess I am.

"Take a breath. We won't hurt your mate. She's safe."

I wrap my arms tightly around Lauren and kiss the top of her head. Her scent soothes me. She's trembling, but to my relief, her arms come around me, and she hugs me back.

"Get that leech away from her," I growl, refusing to look in the direction of the vampire.

He hisses like an angry cat.

"It's all right. We're not going to mind-wipe her. We didn't know she was your mate, son," the sheriff says.

I fight to swallow over the tight band constricting my throat. "She is," I choke. "And I don't care about what that means for your precious gene pool," I say to my dad.

"That's why you've been having episodes." Always the

scientist. He doesn't weigh in about matters of the heart. Or fate. Just the logic behind my condition.

"She's my mate," I repeat. "I'll burn this town to the ground if anyone tries to stand between us."

Lauren's heart thuds against my chest. She slowly pulls back from me to look up. I cradle her beautiful face. "I'm sorry I hurt you today," I murmur, even though everyone in the room has supernatural hearing.

"Clyde, apologies for the assault. I think you understand a wolf will do anything to defend his fated mate if he believes she's in danger." Sheriff Gleason attempts to soothe the vampire now, leading him out of the interrogation room. "We didn't know she was his mate, or we wouldn't have tried to wipe her mind. We will still pay your fee, of course." The men file out, leaving me alone with Lauren.

"What did they do to you?" I choke out, examining my girl for bruises.

A sheen of tears makes her teal eyes bright, but she doesn't cry. "Nothing. I didn't let them do anything." Her voice is strong. "I mean, he momentarily immobilized my muscles, but I fought it off. I put my head down on the table, so he couldn't see my eyes, and I refused to answer any of their questions."

My chest, which has been constricted since the moment Lincoln told me they'd taken Lauren, starts to let in some air. "That's my girl. So fucking strong." I cup her nape and knead the tension away.

She gives my shoulder pad a light shake. "Did you miss your game for me?"

"I don't care about the game. I've been trying to get to you all afternoon. I had another seizure after school on my way to your house, and then I didn't wake up until right before the game because my dad gave me a tranquilizer.

Lauren—I was such a dick. I'm so sorry for how I acted today. If you give me another chance, I will tell the whole fucking school how much you mean to me, and I will never, ever treat you that way again."

Lauren grabs my head and pulls my mouth down to hers. I kiss her hard at first—my wolf frantic to mate tongues with her, then I slow down and go deep.

She breaks the kiss and gives me a slow, knowing smile. "I'll think about it."

Chapter Twenty-One

Lauren

"Lauren!" Lincoln appears in the doorway.

"You can't be back there!" A female voice says–the deputy at the desk, I think.

I turn in Abe's arms.

"What happened?" Lincoln takes in the broken door with wide eyes.

"Um, long story."

"Yeah, let's get out of here." Abe catches my hand and hurries me out the door. As we fast-walk our way past the vampire, sheriff, and Abe's dad and out the door, Abe explains, "Lincoln told me they took you, and that's why I left the game. He drove me here."

"Seriously—what happened?" Lincoln repeats. The Tesla is parked in front, and we all beeline for it.

"It was a misunderstanding," Abe says. He glances my way for back up. "Just...something went down at our family cabin, and my dad thought Lauren knew something about it."

Accurate.

"Because you led him to believe that?" Lincoln accuses.

"No," I cut in. "Truly a misunderstanding."

We climb into the Tesla, Abe tugging me into the back seat with him, so Lincoln is like our chauffeur. "Abe, is the game still going? Let's get you back there."

"No." He pulls me right up against his side, pressing his nose against my hair and inhaling deeply. "I need to be with my girl right now."

"Abe, this is your future. Didn't you say there are talent scouts coming? Lincoln, drive back to the game. *Hurry!*"

Lincoln steps on the accelerator, and the Tesla surges forward. He loves to speed.

"Fine." Abe pulls me onto his lap, his hands sliding up and down my thighs. "But you're mine after the game. If Coach doesn't kill me when I get there."

Lincoln races down the roads like we're in a James Bond movie. I hang onto Abe, who hangs onto me, and we get there in less than six minutes.

"I'll see you after the game." Abe kisses me, hard. "You're staying right?"

I laugh. "Yes, I'm staying."

"Because I'm not done apologizing." He's already jogging away backward. "You're my girl." He points at me.

"We'll see," I say, even though I am one hundred percent on board with Abe Oakley. "Go! Go and kick some ass out there!"

He grins as he turns, running like a demon to the locker rooms and out on the field. Lincoln and I follow through the spectator entrance. It's the middle of the final quarter. Hard to believe because it feels like an eternity has passed since they took me away from here.

But Abe came for me. He *did* fight for me.

For us.

He told his dad I'm his mate—whatever that means.

Lincoln goes up to sit with Rayne, but I don't bother grabbing a seat. I walk down the stairs and stand near the wall overlooking the field at the far sidelines.

Abe is over by the coach, clearly getting chewed out. The coach's head comes up and both of them look our way.

I wave.

The coach stares a moment, then stares a moment, then lifts a hand.

Everyone in the stadium—I swear to God—turns to look my way.

Abe runs out to the field. His teammates shake their heads, hands on hips, like they're mad at him, but as soon as they begin to play, it's clear the Wolf Ridge High team functions as one organism. A synchronized team. A pack. With only nine minutes left on the clock, they run a perfect play in which Abe throws a forty yard pass. Asher catches it and scores the touchdown.

Abe steals the ball next play and throws to J. J., who scores again. Wolf Ridge High scores four more times, creaming their opponents and looking like experienced NFL players rather than teenagers. If there really are three scouts in the stands tonight, they're going to be impressed.

Now I get it—Wolf Ridge football is all just for show. None of it is real because these players are superhuman. Tonight they needed to show off, and they did.

For the first time since we moved here, I cheer for their win.

The moment the clock runs out, Wolf Ridge players go nuts celebrating—throwing each other into the air and doing back flips. Abe comes running straight for me, though. He points his finger at me. "You," he shouts, "are mine." He points his finger at his chest.

Half of the Wolf Ridge fans look my way again.

"You hear that?" he bellows, whipping his helmet from his head and spinning it around. "Lauren Sterling is mine. Bow down to your fucking queen!"

"Cocky much?" I call back.

He stands below me, looking up. "Jump, my queen."

I laugh, throwing a leg over the rail. "You want me to jump?" I sit on the railing, looking down. He's not as far down as he was when I jumped off the cliff, but he's still a good ten feet.

I don't care. I feel invincible when I'm with Abe. I push off the railing, throwing myself forward and screaming as I fall.

He catches me easily in a honeymoon carry, spinning me around. "I need to get my dick inside you right now, princess," he murmurs against my ear.

"I might feel better about that statement if you had showered."

Abe tosses me five feet in the air and catches me again. "Wanna shower with me?"

"Not with the team."

Abe snorts. "I would kill every one of those fuckers if they saw you naked."

I laugh.

Abe carries me straight out to the parking lot, not stopping to talk to the team, get his clothes, or shower.

"Where are we going?"

Abe stops short, and I realize his dad has parked Abe's Range Rover up front and is standing beside it.

"You played," his dad says.

"Yeah."

Abe's dad lifts a hand to me. "Lauren, I'm sorry about earlier. I didn't know you were Abe's mate."

"She doesn't know what that means, Dad." The muscles

under one of Abe's eyes begin to tic. I can tell by the way he blinks hard, he's having trouble seeing again.

"Put me down. I can drive," I say in a low voice.

For once, Abe doesn't front. He doesn't pretend it isn't happening. He sets me on my feet and follows my lead.

"It's happening again," Abe's dad deduces. He opens the passenger side door.

"Yeah." Abe climbs in.

I hold my hand out for the keys, and Abe's dad gives them to me. His eyes are troubled. "If he has another seizure, call me right away. I'm hoping...nevermind. Just go. You two need to be together."

I nod, swallowing. Some of the buoyancy escapes my chest.

"You okay?" I ask when I get behind the wheel. I adjust the seat forward.

"Yeah." Abe's voice is taut. "Can you drive to the cabin?"

"Yes." I start the car. I put it in gear and follow the line of cars out of the parking lot.

Abe covers his eyes even though it's dark out. "Lauren."

I turn out of the lot and drive up the road that winds toward my house. "Yeah?"

Abe slumps in his seat.

"You okay?"

Abe's body starts convulsing. His head falls against my shoulder, and he draws in a sharp breath and straightens himself, coming out of it.

"Fuck."

"Abe, did you just have another seizure?"

His legs jerk out and kick the car. "Lauren." His breath seems labored.

"What is it, Abe?" Panic starts to rise in me. "What are you trying to tell me?"

He starts to convulse again.

I wrench the wheel and skid to a stop on the side of the road. "Abe! Abe! Please."

Abe's eyes glow ice blue. "Lauren." He reaches for me but ends up slumping over, his shaking head dropping to my shoulder.

"That's okay." I rush to unbuckle his seatbelt, to make him comfortable. "You're okay, Abe." I pull his head into my lap and stroke his hair. My heart pounds. I'm ice cold. Tears spear my eyes. "Please be okay."

His body jerks and twitches. His fingers close around my thigh. He turns his head, and I see gleaming canines. Not human-sized. Wolf-sized.

I scream. His teeth bite into my inner thigh, puncturing my flesh.

My body jerks along with Abe's now—a wild convulsing. Not painful.

Pleasurable.

Like an orgasm. His teeth are locked in my inner thigh, and I come and come in the most powerful orgasm of my life.

* * *

Abe

Everything was black. I must have lost consciousness, and then suddenly, I wake up to my face between Lauren's legs. The scent of her arousal brings me around like smelling salts. The pain is gone behind my eyes. The muscles around my eyes rest. In fact, my whole body relaxes and opens like I've just had sex.

But there's blood. Lauren's blood is in my mouth. I gasp, sitting upright. My vision is crystal clear, even in the darkness.

I bit Lauren.

I *marked* Lauren.

Without her consent.

I put my hand over the puncture marks on her thigh, applying pressure to stop the bleeding. "Oh shit. Are you okay, baby? I didn't mean to do that. Oh, fate, Lauren. I'm so sorry."

"What happened?" She looks dazed, but not afraid. Not in pain. No, her face is flushed, her eyes glassy in the same incredible way she looks after I've brought her orgasm.

"I-I marked you, baby. Male wolf shifters bite their mates to embed their scent in her flesh. I guess I lost control while I was seizing."

She doesn't seem fazed by that. "It's weird." She sounds blissed out. Like she's on drugs. "The bite hurt. I mean, it should have hurt. But it doesn't. It feels good. Maybe I really am a masochist."

My dick punches out against my football uniform pants. I slowly lower my head, holding her gaze to make sure she's on board. "Well, I'd better lick the wound."

"You'd better." Her voice is husky. She pushes my head down and spreads her thighs wide.

I rub her pussy through her panties as I lick the wound clean. She writhes her cute little hips in a grinding motion.

I lift my head and lick my lips. There's something different about her blood. Something changed slightly in her scent. "Lauren..."

She presses her fingers over mine between her legs, urging me on.

"You taste like...you taste like a bear."

She stops writhing and gasps. "The bear!" she exclaims. "What is it?"

"That old bear shifter brought me bear brush tea in the hospital."

"What?" I stare at her with wide eyes. "You didn't tell me that."

"I know. For some reason, it felt like something to keep to myself."

"If I'm not mistaken, bear brush tea is a folk remedy to help adolescent shifters find their first shift. It's poisonous to wolves, though, so we don't use it."

Lauren's teal eyes grow round. "But it's not poisonous to bears?"

I shake my head slowly. "Lauren...is there a possibility you're part bear?"

"I felt great after I drank the tea. Strong and alive. That's when I came out and asked you to take me home. And my foot healed much faster than it should have."

I nod. "Thomas must have smelled or tasted it. That's why he double crossed me. Your blood must've tasted good to him. Remember what he said when we were leaving?"

Lauren shakes her head. "Something crazy like, *Do you know what happens when you cross a wolf with a bear?*"

"Maybe that's why that old bear was hanging around. He knew you were one of his kind."

Lauren gasps. "My grandma!"

"You think she was a bear?"

"No. But she came to Arizona on a road trip after college. And supposedly, she loved bears."

"You think she met a bear shifter out here?"

"That's exactly what I think."

"So that old bear..."

"Could be my grandfather!"

I look down at the wounds on her leg. They're already closed. The bleeding stopped. She definitely has shifter healing. "I mated a bear." I grin.

"Didn't the vampire say it's forbidden?"

"Yeah. He said it's because the resulting offspring are dangerous. But we'll figure it out. You know what else is weird?"

"That you biting me turned me on?"

I give her a feral grin and bring my fingers back between her legs. "No, I fucking love that." I stroke along her damp panties. "Mating bites usually happen during climax. But Lauren, I can see perfectly right now. No headache, no distortion."

"Because you marked me?"

I nod. "What if you just cured me, Princess?"

Her lips curve in a seductive smile. "I think we should keep practicing to be sure. Can you mark me more than once?"

"I'm gonna mark every inch of you, Pearls. Just wait until I get you naked."

* * *

Lauren

"*Mine.*" Abe's growl is feral. The shower in the cabin is small, but that doesn't stop him from slamming my naked body up against the wall and licking every inch of me under the spray of water.

I take my turn, pushing him roughly back against the opposite wall. With a soapy palm, I give him a handjob, loving the way his eyes glow and teeth descend as he gets more and more turned on. I work my fist up and down his cock, faster and faster until he snarls and takes back the control.

He spins me around and presses my face against the tile. He's rough with me now that he knows I have bear blood–manhandling me even more than he did before. He strokes my ass, sliding his soapy fingers between my cheeks. "I'm going to fuck this pretty ass soon, Princess."

The part of me that is used to sparring with Abe wants to challenge that statement, but his erotic touch feels too good. My hormones are in overdrive right now. I can't get enough of Abe–his body, his touch, his deep growly voice.

I spread my legs wider and push my ass back at him.

"Fuck," Abe mutters. He winds his hand in my wet hair and pulls my head back. It's rough. Feral. Godly.

I want more. I want everything Abe Oakley has to offer.

He rubs the head of his cock along my pussy then pushes in. With one arm wrapped around my waist to hold me in place, he thrusts in, lifting me off my toes with each powerful buck. He's not gentle–he's a rutting beast.

"You want me to mark you again, Princess?" His voice is guttural.

I love that he asks for permission, even when he's rough. "Yes."

I'm dying for him to mark me again. I can't wait to find out if it makes me come like it did last time.

He continues thrusting so hard I'm sure he'll turn me inside out. Just when I'm about to cry mercy, he thrusts in deep and bites my shoulder.

It's incredible.

Fireworks explode behind my eyes. My entire body convulses again. I rocket into outer space, pleasure blooming from my core outward.

Vaguely, I'm aware of Abe carrying me out of the shower, wrapping me in a towel and bringing me to the bedroom. I'm still in bliss-land, though. Still coming down from the highest high of my life.

I'm a rag doll when he arranges me on the bed–my limbs heavy, muscles loose. He pulls the covers around me and curls up behind me, spoon-style.

"Do bears mark their mates?" I mumble.

"She-bears don't do the marking, sweetheart."

"I might still try."

Abe rolls me over to face him. "Give it to me, Pearls. I want those teeth in my flesh. I want those nails in my back. I want to hear you scream like you just did for the rest of my life."

"Did I scream?" I murmur sleepily.

Abe brushes my cheek with his large thumb. "Yeah. It was awesome." His grin is boyish and sweet.

I reach out and touch his face, too. "Tell me what it means to be your mate."

His eyes glow for a moment, but he blinks it away. "It means you're mine."

I smile. "Interesting theory."

He takes my hand and drags it to his chest. "No, really, Pearls. It means this heart beats for you. For the rest of my life, there will be no one but you. Your happiness, your satisfaction, your orgasms will be all I work for."

I let out a soft laugh. "No, for real."

"That's for real. Wolves mate for life. I permanently embedded my scent in your skin." He traces the fresh wounds on my shoulder. "Twice. Every other shifter will know you've been claimed. You're mine, and I'll kill any other male who tries to take you from me."

I blink. "Okay, that's intense."

"You're the mate Fate chose for me. The only one I will ever feel this way about. It's no wonder you showing up at

Wolf Ridge caused my nervous system to go haywire. It's also no wonder that marking you fixed it."

I trace his eyebrow with my fingertip. "You still feel good? No more headaches or eye problems?"

"I feel incredible. Say you'll be mine, Lauren. I will never deny what you mean to me again."

My chest feels warmer than an oven. After losing my mom, the promise of forever with someone has a huge appeal. It also feels like she somehow led me here. To this. She wanted us to come to Arizona.

I don't know whether she knew about the bear thing or not–I may never know–but she brought us to this place. To the magic.

To Abe.

"I'll be yours," I murmur.

Abe takes my face in both his hands and kisses me. It's a slow but deep kiss. A beautiful kiss. A promise and a discovery.

Epilogue

be

"Geronimo!" I shout, running and leaping off the roof of the Sterling Mansion into the pool far below. The deep, kidney-shaped pool was clearly designed to blend into the landscape, with a built-in waterfall crafted from the boulders found right on the mountainside.

The water splashes out onto the pebblestone deck, making our classmates shout and groan.

Lauren and Lincoln are hosting a pool party, and everyone in the in-crowd—and even quite a few outside of it—are here. In fact, it seems like the party at Sterling Mansion is the social event of the season. Bigger, even, than Homecoming or a full moon run.

Everyone has been curious about the mansion on Moongaze Hill, and now that I've claimed Lauren, she and her brother are their new fascination. Even more after I let out that she's part bear.

That fact also made it easy for my parents to fully embrace her as my mate although my dad did warn that pregnancy could be difficult for her. He thinks the fact that she's part human will mitigate the risks of a bear-wolf breeding, though. Not that we plan to start a family anytime soon.

Lauren and Lincoln's dad stands out on the deck above us. "All right. No more jumping from the roof," he calls out.

He's not in a robe. He's freshly shaven and fully dressed, playing host to my parents and a few other Wolf Ridge luminaries. Something about Lauren coming back to the living breathed life back into him, as well. Lauren says he's working again, and he's started to get to know the people in Wolf Ridge. She and Lincoln are overjoyed at the change in him.

Asher's staring up at the deck with a ferocious glare. I look back up to see what has his wolf riled. I don't see Alpha Green, who Asher will probably always hate for banishing his dad. Who else, then? It's my parents, Wilde's dad and Rayne's mom, Mr. and Mrs. James and—*oh.*

I study Asher's scowl again.

Yep. He's looking at Carlotta James, our former babysitter—the hot she-wolf who haunted all of our middle school pubescent dreams. She's back after graduating from college, and word is she's filling in at Wolf Ridge High for a human teacher on medical leave.

Huh. Interesting. I'm not sure what Asher's hang-up is with her, but I intend to find out.

Lincoln is in a chaise lounge surrounded by a half-dozen she-wolves from Wolf Ridge High. We haven't told him anything—not about his bear blood nor what I am—but we plan to when we decide he needs to know.

We looked for the old bear, but it seems he left Wolf Ridge. No one has caught his scent or seen him. Lauren told me about the last time she saw him, and we agreed it seemed like a goodbye. Like once he knew she was safe, he moved on.

"My turn!" Lauren yells from the rooftop and leaps.

"I said no more!" her dad calls out as she plummets into the water.

I catch my stunning mate, both of us plunging toward the floor of the pool together. I kick hard to swim to the surface with her in my arms, and the two of us mate mouths before we rise, so we come out of the water in a kiss.

We're greeted by a chorus of "Awws" from the party-goers.

"That was magnificent, Pearls."

She tosses her head, her teal eyes dancing. "So fun. Too bad it freaks my dad out."

"You're magnificent," I tell her. It's true. She's incredible. Smart, strong, beautiful. Fate sent me the best possible match.

I never get enough of this girl. She's in a lime green string bikini that makes it challenging for me not to have a continuous hard-on at this party. But then, that's a constant around her.

My eyes are no longer a problem, though. My dad thinks Lauren's bear blood might be part of what healed me, or it could have just been a good old-fashioned love healing. One heart finding its match.

Two damaged souls coming together to become whole again. No, to become so much more than we were before.

I carry her to the pool stairs and exit the pool with her still in my arms, earning another chorus of sighs from our friends.

"Your party is a hit, Pearls. You're their queen now."

She kisses me.

"You're my queen."

"Don't think I'm ever going to call you my king, Abe Oakley."

I grin at her. "Everyone already knows I'm the alpha king here."

She kisses me again, her expression softening. "I love you, Alpha King," she murmurs.

"You're the reason my heart beats, Pearls. I live for you. I love you. And you're mine."

* * *

Dearest reader, thank you so much for reading Alpha King! The next book in the series is Alpha Varsity.

If you enjoyed it, I would so appreciate your reviews, they make a huge difference to indie authors.

Please **join my newsletter for word on new releases: https://subscribepage.com/ alphastemp**. I would also love to see you in my Facebook group, Renee's Romper room. You can order signed paperbacks, get Wolf Ridge t-shirts and stickers at https://shop. reneeroseromance.com/

Want FREE Renee Rose books?

Go to http://subscribepage.com/alphastemp to sign up for Renee Rose's newsletter and receive a free copy of *Alpha's Temptation, Theirs to Protect, Owned by the Marine, Theirs to Punish, The Alpha's Punishment, Disobe-*

dience at the Dressmaker's and *Her Billionaire Boss*. In addition to the free stories, you will also get special pricing, exclusive previews and news of new releases.

Other Titles by Renee Rose

Paranormal

Wolf Ridge High Series

Alpha Bully

Alpha Knight

Step Alpha

Alpha King

Alpha Varsity

Bad Boy Alphas Series

Alpha's Temptation

Alpha's Danger

Alpha's Prize

Alpha's Challenge

Alpha's Obsession

Alpha's Desire

Alpha's War

Alpha's Mission

Alpha's Bane

Alpha's Secret

Alpha's Prey

Alpha's Sun

Shifter Ops

Alpha's Moon

Alpha's Vow

Alpha's Revenge

Alpha's Fire

Alpha's Rescue

Alpha's Command

Werewolves of Wall Street

Big Bad Boss: Midnight

Big Bad Boss: Moon Mad

Big Bad Boss: Marked

Big Bad Boss: Mated

Two Marks Series

Untamed

Tempted

Desired

Enticed

Wolf Ranch Series

Rough

Wild

Feral

Savage

Fierce

Ruthless

Alpha Doms Series

The Alpha's Hunger

The Alpha's Promise

Her Royal Master

Yes, Doctor

Her Russian Master

Her Marine Master

Her Fire Master

Her Hollywood Master

Her Stepbrother Master

Made Men Series

Don't Tease Me

Don't Tempt Me

Don't Make Me

Alpha Mountain

Hero

Rebel

Warrior

Chicago Sin

Den of Sins

Rooted in Sin

Double Doms Series

Theirs to Punish

Theirs to Protect

Holiday Feel-Good

Scoring with Santa

Saved

Other Contemporary

Black Light: Valentine Roulette

Black Light: Roulette Redux

Black Light: Celebrity Roulette

Black Light: Roulette War

Black Light: Roulette Rematch

Punishing Portia (written as Darling Adams)

The Professor's Girl

Safe in his Arms

Sci-Fi
Zandian Masters Series

His Human Slave

His Human Prisoner

Training His Human

His Human Rebel

His Human Vessel

His Mate and Master

Zandian Pet

Their Zandian Mate

His Human Possession

Zandian Brides

Night of the Zandians

Bought by the Zandians

Mastered by the Zandians

Zandian Lights

Kept by the Zandian

Claimed by the Zandian

Stolen by the Zandian

Rescued by the Zandian

Other Sci-Fi

The Hand of Vengeance

Her Alien Masters

About Renee Rose

USA TODAY BESTSELLING AUTHOR RENEE ROSE loves a dominant, dirty-talking alpha hero! She's sold over two million copies of steamy romance with varying levels of kink. Her books have been featured in USA Today's *Happily Ever After* and *Popsugar*. Named Eroticon USA's Next Top Erotic Author in 2013, she has also won *Spunky and Sassy's* Favorite Sci-Fi and Anthology author, *The Romance Reviews* Best Historical Romance, and has hit the *USA Today* list fifteen times with her Bad Boy Alphas, Chicago Bratva, and Wolf Ranch series.

Renee loves to connect with readers!
www.reneeroseromance.com
reneeroseauthor@gmail.com

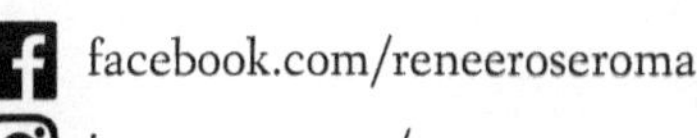

facebook.com/reneeroseromance
instagram.com/reneeroseromance
bookbub.com/authors/renee-rose